Voyage Throughout Planet Guoke

Inspired by the True Experiences of

Zhang XiangQian

Alexandria, Virginia, USA

By Hope Grace

Published by Hope Grace Publishing 2025
HopeGracePublishing.com
Alexandria, Virginia, USA

This is a work of fiction. Names, characters, places, and incidents are either the product of the author's imagination or used fictitiously. Any resemblance to actual events, locales, or persons, living or dead, is entirely coincidental.

ISBN: 978-1-966423-00-3 (Paperback)
ISBN: 978-1-966423-13-3 (Hardback)
ISBN: 978-1-966423-01-0 (eBook)

Library of Congress Control Number:
2024925068

First Edition: 2025

Contents

Preface

Voyage Throughout Planet Guoke is a novel inspired by the real-life experiences of Zhang XiangQian. While the characters and events within these pages are fictional, the portrayal of Guoke Planet and its extraordinary technologies is grounded in Zhang's personal encounters and insights. For those interested in a deeper exploration of alien technology, Zhang has also published United Field Theory (Academic Edition) – Extraterrestrial Technology. Readers who wish to learn more about the technologies described in this novel may find additional insights in that work.

At its heart, this novel blends science fiction with philosophical exploration, pushing the boundaries of our understanding of technology, identity, and human experience. Guoke Planet introduces readers to advanced innovations — from instantaneous transport to body replication and consciousness transfer — inviting us to consider the potential of such developments in our own reality.

But beyond the marvels of technology, this story delves into the complex, often unsettling relationship between humans and the unknown. Zhang's journey is not merely one of discovery; it is a confrontation with profound questions about existence, relationships, and the merging of mind, body, and machine. His encounters with the inhabitants of Guoke Planet test the very essence of what it means to be human.

While the narrative takes creative liberties to craft a thrilling and immersive world, the essence of Guoke Planet's technologies — their vision, power, and potential—remains rooted in Zhang's own experiences. This journey serves as the foundation for the tale, blending fact with fiction to explore the limits of our universe and the mind.

It is my hope that you, the reader, will find as much fascination and wonder in Guoke Planet as Zhang did on his remarkable journey. Prepare for a voyage where the lines between imagination and reality blur. Welcome to a world of extraordinary possibilities — both beautiful and unsettling.

Enjoy the voyage!

Chapter 1: Taken from Home

The night I left home was like no other. It wasn't through the front door that I exited my house, but rather through the walls. The Guoke people, as I later came to know them, had ways beyond human comprehension — ways that made ordinary actions extraordinary. They passed through walls like light through glass, and I followed.

The moment my body touched the wall, the smell of damp earth filled my nostrils, leaving a lasting impression. It was not the solid wall cracking open but rather its very molecules shifting and allowing me to pass through. I felt the tiny granules of the wall gently rubbing against me as I moved, a strange but exhilarating sensation. This wasn't a dream; it was real.

Before that, I had sensed something above the roof of my parents' house. Half-asleep, I felt a familiar presence — something I had sensed as a child. Suddenly, the room was flooded with a deep red glow, waking me instantly. I climbed out of bed and saw glowing liquid seeping through the walls. The liquid emitted a reddish light, intertwined with flashes of pale blue, forming uneven clusters of bright, tiny points of light. The liquid gradually coalesced into human-like figures, their bodies flickering as if made from countless tiny, flying red insects.

Fear gripped me as I stood frozen, trembling uncontrollably. My limbs stiffened, and my throat tightened, as though I had lost control of my body. The Guoke people—these mysterious figures— didn't speak, yet I heard a male voice inside my mind, clear and unmistakable: "Come with us."

Before I could process what was happening, an invisible force hit me, taking control of my body. My head felt heavy, as if filled with liquid and sand. My thoughts became slow and muddled, and I couldn't walk steadily. But as I followed them, the fear eased. I watched in astonishment as they passed through the wall, and I followed, seeing the wall turn semi-transparent as we walked right through it.

I emerged outside barefoot, dressed only in a shirt and shorts. The smell of the earth from the wall still lingered in my memory. The sensation of passing through the wall was unlike anything I had ever felt, as if every particle of the wall was slipping through my body. And it wasn't a fast process — just the same pace as walking. For years, I would dream of walking through walls, sometimes succeeding and sometimes failing, and the feeling of crashing into the wall was painfully real.

Once outside, I noticed two more people. One of them held a device that cast light onto the wall, turning it transparent. It struck me then that these people could manipulate both solid and liquid forms at will, their bodies constantly vibrating, giving them an almost unreal quality. I began to suspect that these weren't real people at all — perhaps they were some kind of advanced robots, a suspicion that would later be confirmed

As I stood there, I saw another figure — someone who seemed more real. It was a woman, looking almost human but with features far too delicate and precise. Her skin was an ethereal blend of pink and white, smooth and soft, and her eyes were large and luminous, framed by thin, short eyebrows that arched high, giving her an otherworldly allure. Her hair was black with streaks of pale blue, coiled like rubber tubes, segmented and spiraling out like antennae. Her slender frame seemed impossibly small, her waist no thicker than my arm, yet her hips were wide, giving her an exaggerated hourglass shape. I couldn't help but be mesmerized by her.

Her body was unlike anything I had seen. The proportions were oddly different from humans, her legs spaced further apart than a human's, and her form appeared unnaturally smooth, like a finely sculpted figure. Her clothing was a skintight suit that seemed fused to her body, accentuating every curve as though it were part of her skin. Later I learned that her name was Weili.

My thoughts were interrupted by a strange, focused beam of white light that swept across the ground. It was like nothing I had seen before. The light moved in sections, dense and precise, illuminating objects in its path with crystal clarity but leaving no spillover light in the surrounding area. This was unlike the flashlights we humans use, where light scatters in all directions. The light was so concentrated that it formed no beam in the air, yet everything it touched was perfectly lit.

Looking up, I saw the source of the light: a massive object, shaped like two large, dark hats joined at the brim, hovering silently above. The beam came from its base, and around its edges were faint, flickering lights of different colors. My mind raced. Could this be… a UFO? I had read about them in magazines, but to see one was another thing entirely. This confirmed my growing suspicion— these people were not human. They were aliens.

Before I could fully process what was happening, my body felt light, as if lifted from the ground, and in less than a second, everything around me changed. I wasn't outside my house anymore. I found myself inside a perfectly round room, the walls made of seamless metal, polished and glowing softly. There were no doors, no windows — only the dim, even light that seemed to emanate from the walls themselves. The room was pristine, its design elegant in its simplicity, with only a central pillar and a few sparse objects placed neatly around.

Standing there in shock, I realized that I was aboard their ship. It wasn't just any ship; it was a spacecraft. As I stood in the circular chamber, I watched a 3D hologram flicker to life in front of me. The hologram shifted and changed, showing scenes and figures in stunning detail, as if the images were real.

Then, I noticed four figures, their bodies trembling ever so slightly. They had no expression and seemed almost like they were made from thousands of tiny insects, just like the beings that had appeared in my room. These were not living beings but some kind of advanced robots. Two of them approached me, removing my shirt and shorts in silence, leaving me standing there completely naked. Despite my embarrassment, a soft, floating white mist appeared around my waist, offering me a strange sense of modesty.

As I stood there, I realized that I had truly left my home, taken by these beings—these Guoke people—to a place far beyond anything I could have imagined.

Chapter 2: Conversations During the Flight

Each time I felt my body lighten, I heard a soft, sweet, almost clingy female voice speaking, though I couldn't pinpoint where it came from. It was as if it was directly in my mind, whispering continuously. A three-dimensional virtual screen in front of me briefly showed a planet before it vanished. Occasionally, I saw diagrams indicating our path, sometimes zigzagging through space. When I closed my eyes, it felt as though the craft had disappeared, leaving me floating alone in the vast, dark void of the universe, slowly falling into an endless abyss. The sensation was terrifying, and I had to open my eyes to escape it.

After the ship began its journey, the task of navigating was handed over to the robotic entities. They monitored the 3D virtual screens as they operated the ship. With nothing else to do, we began talking. I was most curious about the ship we were on—the infamous "flying saucer" often mentioned on Earth.

"This craft we're on, it's what we Earthlings call a 'flying saucer,' right?" I asked.

"Yes, that's correct," said Sudair, one of my companions.

"Flying saucers are said to travel incredibly fast. I read in a magazine that they can reach the speed of light, about 300,000 kilometers per second. Is that true?"

"Yes, flying saucers can travel at the speed of light," Sudair explained. "In fact, our saucers operate in three different space-time states. The first is what we call the 'zero-mass excitation state,' where the saucer's mass becomes zero, and it moves at light speed, much like the light waves in nature. The second state is a 'quasi-excitation state,' where the saucer has a very small mass, about one ten-thousandth of a gram. In this state, it can hover, move at any speed below light speed, and even float in the air on planets like Earth. It can also switch to zero-mass and reach light speed at any time. The third state is the 'normal state,' where the saucer is stationary, its mass is constant, and its internal systems are turned off."

I was intrigued by how simple it seemed. "If the saucer's flying principle is so straightforward, what makes it work? How does it achieve zero mass?" I asked.

Sudair responded, "The principle is actually quite simple. In your language, it can be described in a single sentence: 'Any object in the universe, if you reduce its mass to zero, will immediately begin moving at the speed of light.' That's the core principle of how our saucers achieve light-speed travel."

This explanation caught me off guard. It seemed too simple. But how could they make an object's mass reach zero? That was the real question. Sudair continued, sensing my confusion.

"There are two types of movement in the universe: quantitative change and qualitative change. Ordinary motion, such as what you observe with cars and planes on Earth, is a form of quantitative change. Your scientists like Newton and Galileo have done well to explain this type of movement. Earth-based vehicles follow the principle of momentum, where force is the rate of change of momentum over time. On Earth, momentum is calculated as mass times velocity."

He paused before continuing, "But on our planet, momentum is calculated differently. It's the difference between the speed of light and the object's velocity, multiplied by the object's mass. And when we calculate the change of momentum over time, it results in four fundamental forces, which are derived from the changing mass and speed of the object.

Sudair then added, "The saucer's speed doesn't change continuously. When its mass reaches zero, it suddenly jumps to light speed. This instantaneous change is one of the reasons our saucers can travel such vast distances in such a short time."

I tried to absorb this information. It seemed that the saucer's speed depended on its mass, and when the mass reached zero, the speed jumped to light speed. But I had to ask, "Even if your saucers travel at the speed of light, it should still take years to travel between distant planets. How can you reach your home planet in just a few hours?"

Norton, another one of my companions, smiled and explained, "When an object moves at light speed, the length of space in the direction of travel becomes zero."

I was shocked. "So, the space you travel through essentially collapses?"

Sudair clarified further, "Yes, exactly. To put it in simpler terms, the farther we travel at light speed, the shorter the distance becomes. You've heard the phrase 'far yet near'? That's the principle at work."

I was astounded by this idea, but still, there was a lingering question. "If space in the direction of travel shortens to zero, then doesn't that mean you don't need any time to travel? Why, then, does it still take you several hours to return to your planet?"

Norton explained, "While it's true that in the light-speed state, travel through space seems instantaneous, the process of transitioning between different space-time states—like reducing the saucer's mass to zero and back—takes time. For instance, when we first launch, we reduce the saucer's mass gradually. When we arrive, we increase the mass again. This process, called 'state conversion,' is what takes time, not the actual travel."

Sudair added, "When we reach your planet, the saucer doesn't return to its full mass immediately. We keep it at small mass to conserve energy. The real time it takes is in converting between states, especially when we need to avoid large objects like planets."

"So, flying around stars and planets adds to the time it takes?" I asked.

"Yes," Norton confirmed. "Our saucer uses an energy field to reduce its mass during flight. But when we encounter large objects like planets, we have to avoid them or risk colliding. To do this, we switch states. This state conversion is what takes time during our journey."

I was beginning to understand. The flight didn't take time because of the distance—it took time because of the need to convert between different space-time states. But the concept of reducing mass and traveling at light speed still felt beyond my understanding.

Then, I asked a question that had been bothering me for a while: "If your saucers can accelerate so quickly, how do you prevent the passengers from experiencing extreme forces? Wouldn't they be crushed by the sudden acceleration?"

Sudair smiled, "Our saucers fly with zero or very small mass, so the passengers don't feel any force. No matter how fast we accelerate, the forces remain negligible. That's why our ships are silent and have no friction with the air—they aren't interacting with the atmosphere like your airplanes do."

This explanation made sense to me, but I still had more questions. "How do you make these saucers? What kind of power source do they use?"

Norton answered, "We use energy from nuclear or neutron sources, but remember, the saucer itself doesn't need power during long-distance flights. It uses inertia. The energy is only needed for the initial state conversion, when the saucer's mass is reduced."

The conversation continued as they explained the complexities of the saucer's construction, its round shape, and its ability to move in various directions, even in Earth's atmosphere. The more I learned, the more I realized how advanced the Guoke people's technology was. They weren't just traveling through space—they were manipulating space and time themselves.

Chapter 3: Guoke Planet's Faster-Than-Light Communication

We fell silent for a while before I suddenly thought of another question. "How do you control the flying saucer?" I asked.

"The saucer's speed is too fast for any living being to pilot it manually. All our saucers are controlled by pre-programmed computer systems," Sudair explained. "There's also a difference in how time flows inside and outside the saucer. The internal and external time-space aren't the same, and even different sections of the saucer experience different time flows. For example, the section where the controls are located operates on a different time scale than the rest of the ship."

Sudair continued, "Before we can travel to a specific planet, we first measure its distance and coordinates relative to ours. Then, we input the exact flight time required to cover that distance into the control system. Once the program is set, the saucer can begin its journey. When we approach Earth, we bring the saucer into a quasi-excitation state, allowing it to hover. Then, to cover shorter distances, we switch the saucer into a light-speed mode for a very brief moment. By continuously switching between these states, the saucer can fly at any speed we choose, far below the speed of light, and maneuver in Earth's atmosphere."

I thought about the precision needed for such journeys. "So, if the measurements aren't accurate, wouldn't that cause a crash?"

"Exactly," Sudair nodded. "If the measurements are off, it's like your airplanes crashing into mountains. The saucer could collide with a planet, resulting in complete destruction. That's why we rely on pre-programmed settings. The saucer approaches Earth at light speed and, as we near the planet, switches to a state where it moves at much slower speeds."

He added, "But measuring distances isn't a challenge for us. On Earth, your most advanced tool for measurement is the laser. We use something far more advanced—an artificial field. This field is a cylindrical, spiral-moving space that can measure far more accurately than any laser."

I was curious about this "field" he kept mentioning. "Doesn't measurement involve transmitting information? On Earth, we use lasers to measure the distance to the Moon by bouncing the beam back to Earth. But isn't that method limited by distance and speed?"

Sudair responded, "Indeed. Lasers have significant limitations. They lose energy over long distances and are constrained by the speed of light. But with our artificial field, energy loss is nearly zero, allowing us to measure planets much farther away. The field itself moves faster than light, because it's not a physical entity like photons—it's space itself, which isn't restricted by the speed of light."

I was stunned by this revelation. Faster-than-light communication? That was a game-changer. "So, you not only use this field for measurement but also for communication?" I asked.

"Yes," Sudair confirmed. "We use artificial field scanning for communication, which far surpasses laser or electromagnetic wave communication. Think about how people on Earth use electromagnetic waves to communicate over long distances, even while driving cars. It works because the speed of light is far faster than the speed of a car. But if you're traveling in a light-speed saucer, using light-speed electromagnetic waves to communicate would be pointless. That's why we use faster-than-light communication through the field—it's the only viable option for us."

"Do you use this field-based communication on Guoke Planet as well?" I asked.

"Of course," Sudair replied. "On our planet, we rely entirely on field communication. It's vastly superior to electromagnetic communication. For example, if there's a mining accident deep underground on Earth, electromagnetic signals can't penetrate the thick layers of earth to reach the surface. But our field communication, which uses space itself as the medium, can pass through an entire planet without any obstacles."

He continued, "Not only can we use the field to communicate through solid matter, but it also allows us to observe deep into the universe, even peering into the microscopic world smaller than electrons and photons. It can even help us look inside planets, predicting seismic activity with incredible precision."

Norton joined in, adding, "The beauty of field communication is that it's not limited by the physical properties of matter. The energy loss during transmission is practically zero, allowing it to travel vast distances without weakening. The only energy used is at the points of transmission and reception. Additionally, the speed of transmission is theoretically infinite, unlike electromagnetic waves, which are capped at the speed of light."

I was baffled by this. "How is that possible? According to Earth's understanding of relativity, nothing can move faster than light, right?"

"Space is a unique kind of substance," Sudair explained. "It doesn't have mass or charge like ordinary particles, so it isn't constrained by the same rules. Ordinary particles, when they approach the speed of light, experience an increase in mass, which prevents them from reaching or exceeding light speed. But space itself has no such limitations."

Norton chimed in, "In fact, using space to transmit information is the highest form of communication in the universe. Anything that relies on physical particles is inherently limited. True advancement comes from utilizing space itself for communication."

Sudair continued, "Not only do we use space for communication, but we also use it for large-scale data processing on our planet. Our public information network, like the internet you're beginning to develop, is powered by space. Our computers are virtual, and all communication is conducted through space. With artificial field scanning, every person's brain is constantly connected to others and to the global network, without the need for physical devices. We can communicate, access information, and even 'go online' using only our minds."

I tried to wrap my head around this concept. "So, you store data in space?"

"Yes," Sudair nodded. "Space has an unlimited capacity to store information. According to our understanding of the universe, any point in space can theoretically store all the information of the past, present, and future. While there are some practical limits, the potential of space for storing information is far beyond anything Earth can currently comprehend."

Norton added, "Earthlings are still focused on tangible resources like food, oil, and metals, but eventually, they will realize that information and data are the most valuable assets. When your people develop light-speed travel and enter the era of interstellar exploration, traditional communication methods will no longer suffice. You'll need instant, near-infinite-speed communication like our field-based system."

As the conversation trailed off, the 3D holographic images inside the ship suddenly disappeared. The red, trembling robots shrank down, their bodies becoming tiny purple-red droplets that scattered onto the floor before disappearing into the ship's interior.

Then, that mysterious, soothing voice returned—not in my ears but in my mind—saying, "We've arrived at Guoke Planet. It's time to go down."

Before I even realized it, we had reached their planet. The journey was over. As the others stepped out of the ship, one of them said, "We're here. Let's go down and begin your visit."

Chapter 4: The Saucer Warehouse of Guoke Planet

I was filled with excitement, imagining what this advanced planet might look like. I envisioned a bustling metropolis, with people in cutting-edge, perhaps even strange, futuristic fashion, moving through vibrant streets. Skyscrapers towering into the sky, sleek flying cars zipping overhead — it had to be a spectacle of technological wonder. I even entertained the thought of being greeted by some grand leader or a crowd of cheering citizens.

But as we left the ship, not by walking, but by feeling ourselves gently float out, the scene before me was far from what I had imagined. There was no welcoming crowd, no bustling city streets. Instead, what lay ahead was a massive storage space filled with flying saucers of various sizes, stacked on racks like vehicles in a parking lot.

A few robots were hovering around one saucer, probably the very one we had just flown in. I realized that this must be the flying saucer warehouse.

Now standing close to our ship, I observed its exterior up close. Its metallic hull gleamed in a dull lead-gray, seamless, with no visible welds, windows, or even lights. Yet somehow, it had emitted light. How did that work? The ship had hovered over Earth effortlessly. I guessed that people must enter and exit through the bottom. Inside, the large central pillar was likely hollow, connected to a door at the base.

I noticed another saucer preparing for takeoff. It hovered a meter off the ground, wobbled slightly from side to side as if adjusting its balance, then spun counterclockwise before vanishing in a flash. As I watched, the strange fogginess in my brain faded, and I felt fully alert again, clear-headed.

I looked up and surveyed the immense warehouse. It was enormous, stretching endlessly in every direction. The ceiling seemed to reach as high as a skyscraper, with flying saucers stacked on racks that went up dozens of stories. Standing there, I couldn't help but wonder what kind of material the walls and roof were made of, to support such an enormous structure without a single supporting column. It seemed impossible by Earth's standards.

I also noticed that my body felt heavier than it did on Earth. It took more effort to move, which made me suspect that the planet's gravity was stronger than Earth's. That meant the materials used for the ceiling had to be exceptionally strong to withstand the pressure.

Curiously, I walked over to the warehouse wall and examined it. The surface was smooth, soft, pale yellow, and flawless. It was so refined and perfect that it seemed almost unnecessary for a simple wall to be this well-crafted. Looking closer, I realized it resembled the bodies of the robots—made up of countless tiny particles that shimmered with a faint vibration. These weren't regular vibrations, but chaotic, disorganized ones that gave the wall an almost alive feeling.

I reached out to touch the wall. My hand stopped short, as if repelled by an invisible force. The further I pushed, the stronger the resistance grew, like the feeling of two magnets repelling each other. But the force here was far stronger than anything I had felt before.

"Could this wall be made of some sort of virtual material?" I wondered aloud.

A voice, calm and familiar, appeared in my mind again. "You're right. The wall is a virtual construction generated by an artificial field. The field produces two effects: a planar repulsion field, which pushes everything away, the opposite of Earth's gravity, and a light stabilization field, which solidifies the light within a chosen area. The yellow color you see is the result of solidifying yellow light, while the other colors are filtered out. We could just as easily make it blue, red, or green, depending on the designer's preference."

The voice continued, "The light used for this is gathered from the surrounding environment. At night, when less light is available, the walls would appear dimmer. But this is more than just an illusion. If you were to turn off the artificial field, the walls and ceiling would vanish instantly."

I was stunned. A whole planet with virtual walls? What kind of world had I stepped into?

The voice elaborated further, "The virtual walls and ceiling are just forms of energy. They can withstand impacts much better than physical walls, though they do have limits. If something strikes the virtual structure with enough speed and force, it can break through. The strength of these walls depends entirely on the amount of energy we put into the field."

As I processed this information, the voice added something that truly amazed me: "Our entire planet is highly virtualized."

I never expected that the first incredible thing I would encounter on Guoke Planet would be its virtual walls.

Chapter 5: First Encounter with the Global Public Information Network

"Is your planet in the Milky Way? How far is it from Earth?" I asked in my mind, but this time, there was no answer from the familiar voice.

This voice had followed me ever since I left my home on Earth. Sometimes it felt like a real voice in my ears, while at other times, it was more like a thought that simply appeared in my mind—less a sound and more an impression, as if it didn't come from my ears at all. Was it some kind of translation device they had installed in me? If so, whose words were being translated? Who was speaking to me? And who was answering my questions?

I tried again, "Who are you? I can't see you, yet you're always with me."

Finally, the voice responded, "I am the intelligent system of the QuTu 300, the spacecraft you're currently aboard. I can provide two types of language services remotely: one uses our interception technology, sending signals directly to your brain, and the other transmits sound to your ears."

"So, was it you I heard back at my house on Earth?" I asked.

"Yes, the QuTu 300 was hovering above your home, providing you with language services. Although you are now on our planet, you're still near the QuTu 300, so the ship's systems are continuing to serve you. However, once you step outside this saucer warehouse, the QuTu 300 will no longer be responsible for your information services."

The voice continued, "Our planet has two major networks. The first is the Global Public Movement Network, which allows people and objects to travel across the planet at the speed of light. The second is the Global Public Information Network, which provides information services to everyone on the planet. Once you leave this warehouse, the Global Public Information Network will take over and offer you a range of services. These services include: sending sound information directly into your brain using interception technology, transmitting 3D visual information into your mind, remotely projecting sounds into your ears via artificial field scanning, and generating 3D holographic images in front of you. The system can also read your thoughts remotely and non-invasively."

I was amazed. Their information network was far beyond anything we had on Earth, resembling the internet but taken to a whole new level. Unlike our internet, which relies on physical devices to send information, their Global Public Information Network used space itself to transmit data. Every person on their planet had their brain directly connected to this network.

With this constant connection, they didn't need to memorize information or go through the painstaking process of learning as we do. Whenever they needed knowledge, they simply accessed the network through their minds, much like how we use search engines. However, there was no need for schools, teachers, or even books. In a way, all the people on their planet could share the same pool of knowledge.

For more creative or flexible skills, they used what they called "interception technology." This involved scanning information directly into a person's brain while they slept. A person could wake up the next morning with entirely new knowledge or skills, without ever having to study.

This technology also allowed them to store memories outside their bodies. Their brains could offload information to external storage, much like a cloud system for thoughts. Additionally, they could engage in virtual experiences, whether it was watching movies, playing games, or even interacting with friends—without ever leaving their beds. They could even engage in virtual relationships, including simulated romantic and intimate experiences, using this same interception technology.

I was left speechless, trying to comprehend the full scope of their technological capabilities. What seemed like science fiction on Earth was a daily reality on Guoke Planet.

Chapter 6: Stepping Onto the Streets of Guoke Planet

As soon as we left the flying saucer warehouse, the environment around us shifted dramatically. In an instant, we were standing in the middle of a bustling city street on their planet. But to my surprise, it wasn't anything like what I had imagined.

I expected a futuristic world filled with towering skyscrapers, crowded streets, and strange, cutting-edge technology. Instead, while there were tall buildings—some stretching so high you couldn't see the top — the layout was eerily calm and orderly. The architecture was sleek and minimalist, and the streets were pristine, as if they had never been touched. The road surfaces were a soft bluish green, possibly made of some advanced plastic-like material, and lined with unusual, exotic plants arranged in perfect rows.

But something was missing — there were no cars, no traffic of any kind. There were no airplanes in the sky or even the familiar sight of their flying saucers. I thought perhaps the saucers were simply too fast to be seen. There were also no shops, no hotels, and no signs of the bustling urban life I had anticipated.

Many of the tall buildings had virtual walls, much like the ones I had seen at the saucer warehouse. These walls displayed various colored patterns that seemed to align with where doors and windows would be. I guessed these were part of the virtual buildings' facades, while the real structures were much smaller in comparison. Some buildings even floated in midair, unsupported, with strange shapes — upside-down pyramids, others reaching high into the sky, possibly extending into space itself.

Floating above some of these buildings were large characters, perhaps their written language. The symbols looked like a mix between English and Japanese but were not Chinese. These characters hovered independently in the air, unattached to any structure.

I stood there, looking around, and it finally hit me: this was truly another planet. My last faint hope that I might still be somewhere on Earth dissolved completely. The scene was far too alien for that.

Oddly enough, instead of feeling more nervous, a sense of calm washed over me. I was here now—there was no going back. Just then, the familiar voice in my head changed. It was no longer the deep, calm male voice but a sweet, almost seductive girl's voice, as if she were speaking directly to my heart. Later, I would learn that this voice was generated by their artificial intelligence.

"Welcome, Brother Qian from Earth, to the Guoke Star System," she purred. Her tone was sweet and playful. "The Global Public Information Network of Guoke Star System is here to serve you."

Star system? Why not just call it a planet? I wondered. But before I could ponder that, a three-dimensional hologram of an incredibly beautiful but slightly wicked-looking girl appeared before me. Her sultry voice continued, "I am Kewen, your personal service agent from the Global Public Information Network. Wherever you go on our planet, I will be here to provide you with information and services. I'm your sweet, charming guide…"

The hologram of Kewen smiled as she said, "You're about to explore Guoke Planet, a highly virtualized world, and also…" she leaned in closer as her voice became even more intimate, "…a planet of indulgence, known across the universe for its sensual games."

Wait — did she just say, "planet of indulgence"? I was taken aback. Was that how they introduced their home? I couldn't have misunderstood. It seemed like such a strange and brazen way to describe their world. I didn't fully grasp what she meant at the time, but after spending more time on Guoke, I would come to understand all too well.

Most of the inhabitants of Guoke Planet didn't have to work. Their daily lives revolved around entertainment, particularly elaborate forms of intimate games. It was a leisure-driven society, and though there were many highly advanced planets like Guoke in the universe, each had its own preferred type of game. Here, the focus was on pleasure.

As Kewen spoke, her body began to shrink while moving closer to me, and her clothes seemed to melt away. The hologram grew smaller until it entered my chest and disappeared, leaving behind a faint scent of perfume. Strangely, I could feel something, a brief flutter in my chest. Was it just a virtual image?

I instinctively glanced down to check if the white mist that covered my bare body was still in place, and fortunately, it was. Relieved, I touched my ear again, wondering if there was some kind of translation device implanted there. But there was nothing.

I wanted to find a mirror to see for myself, but I figured it might be awkward to ask, so I let it go.

The sunlight on this planet was brilliant, yet there was a slight chill in the air. Despite the light, the warmth didn't seem to reach my skin. Everything around me was vivid, almost too bright, with exceptional clarity. Even distant objects seemed unnervingly sharp to my eyes. The plants were mostly green, some deep forest green, and a few had a waxy texture. There were no dried or yellow leaves anywhere, and the grass — often pointed and thin on Earth — was entirely absent.

Later, I learned that Guoke Planet orbits a star just like our Sun, but the energy it receives is far less intense than what Earth gets from the Sun. This caused their plants to evolve with more vibrant colors to boost photosynthesis. It also explained why there was so little dust in the air. The atmosphere was so clean that it enhanced the vividness of everything around me.

The ground was spotless. There were no fallen leaves or debris of any kind. Birds, colorful and varied, dotted the landscape, seemingly unafraid of humans. They were everywhere, but strangely, I saw no trace of bird droppings. The base of every tree was wrapped in some sort of material, likely to prevent any debris from falling onto the streets. In densely populated areas, the ground was covered with a plastic-like material that felt durable yet soft underfoot, far more advanced than Earth's cement.

There were no deserts or barren lands on Guoke. Everything was meticulously maintained, even the rivers had artificially built embankments. The air was continually purified, and their entire planet was kept in perfect environmental balance.

Surprisingly, there were few people on the streets. Those I did see moved leisurely, many of them barefoot, as if there was no rush in their world. Some even floated above the ground, hovering a meter off the street as they drifted by.

Everyone looked astonishingly young, around the height of a schoolchild—no one taller than a meter. Their skin was flawless, soft, pale pink without blemishes. The people were beautiful, resembling life-sized porcelain dolls, perfect in every way. But I realized later that their appearance wasn't entirely natural. With their global movement and information networks, they could alter their appearance remotely, like a digital filter on a video.

Their clothing was minimal, just a tight-fitting top and a small skirt. Some skirts were adorned with thin, flowing tubes that swayed as they walked, while others were laced with metallic threads. Their outfits, though simple, looked more like painted-on images than actual fabric. I soon discovered that their clothes were, in fact, virtual projections created by the global networks. None of their clothing was real.

As I continued walking, I noticed that many of the people, both men and women, had strange floating 3D images hovering around their shoulders or above their heads. The images were different for each person — some looked like small animals, others like abstract symbols or machines, and some changed constantly.

Curious, I asked Kewen, "What are those floating images above their heads?"

"That's a virtual signature created by our remote imaging technology," Kewen explained. "It's a form of self-expression or a personal signature, representing the person's mood or personality."

Though I still didn't fully understand, I nodded. "I see… it's like a personal style statement."

Sudair interrupted, "How do you find the air here?"

"It's great," I said, realizing how fresh and clean it felt. "It seems like there's more oxygen in the air than on Earth, right?"

"Yes," Sudair nodded. "But it's not just the oxygen. The key components are negative ions and other gases. We've found that the right balance is crucial for health."

Norton then said, "We should head back to our residence now. We can show you more of our planet later."

"How far is your residence from here?" I asked.

"About 10,000 kilometers by Earth's measurements," Norton replied casually.

"So, what kind of transportation will we use? Are we taking another saucer?" I asked.

No one answered. Instead, Norton raised his hand and made a sharp gesture. Immediately, Kewen's soft voice appeared in my ear, "Request for teleportation: alien humanoid approved."

I felt my body lighten briefly, and in the next moment, I heard the same voice say, "Welcome home!"

In a flash, we had traveled 10,000 kilometers. I hadn't seen a vehicle, no saucer — nothing. Norton had simply waved his hand. My mind filled with questions: What kind of technology could do this? And how did it work so effortlessly?

Chapter 7: Experiencing Teleportation and the Global Public Movement Network

We arrived directly inside Norton's home, not by walking through a door like on Earth, but by simply appearing there, almost as if reality itself bent around us. It was as if one moment we were somewhere else, and the next, we were inside. The home was incredibly clean and modern, filled with both virtual and physical elements. Virtual walls, a virtual bed, and a virtual sofa sat alongside a tangible table — one of the few solid objects.

Weili, Norton, and Sudair had all accompanied me back from Earth. As I took in my surroundings, I couldn't help but notice Weili's calm but sharp gaze. She had been with Norton and Sudair when they came to get me. Unlike the others, though, she radiated an energy that was quiet yet intense, like she knew more than she let on.

We sat down on the virtual sofa, and to my surprise, it felt like sitting on air — light, but still comfortable, as though an invisible force was supporting me. Curious, I got up and moved to bed, testing it. It too was soft and welcoming.

"If you turn this bed off, what happens?" I asked aloud, still baffled by how virtual objects could feel so real.

"You'll fall to the ground," Sudair said with a mischievous grin. And just like that, he did something that made the bed vanish, and I dropped on the floor. Even though the fall wasn't far, being naked made it sting more than it should have. I quickly scrambled up, trying to pretend it didn't hurt.

"Not funny," Weili chided softly, giving Sudair a disapproving look. Her voice, though gentle, carried an undertone of authority that could make anyone take her seriously.

Weili had been there from the beginning, one of the three who had come to take me from Earth. She had been with Norton and Sudair when they approached me, her presence always understated but powerful. From the moment we met, there was something about her that felt different. She wasn't just another figure in this alien landscape—she had purpose, and I could sense it, though she hadn't yet revealed what it was.

Unlike Norton and Sudair, who openly discussed their plans and explained their technology, Weili remained quiet, always observing. Yet, there was a connection between us, something unspoken but undeniably real. She knew from the start why I had been taken, both for the scans they wanted to conduct on my brain and for the more intimate experiments involving my physical and mental reactions to their females. She had known all of this, yet there was no judgment in her eyes. Instead, she seemed to be carefully watching, as if trying to understand me better, perhaps even protecting me in her own way.

I returned to the virtual sofa, still slightly on edge after my fall. Weili sat beside me, her presence somehow both comforting and mysterious.

"Feeling heavy?" she asked, her voice soft but probing, as if she already knew the answer.

"Yeah, ever since I arrived, everything feels heavier. It's like the gravity here is stronger," I replied, shifting uncomfortably. Despite the virtual mist surrounding me, I couldn't shake the awkwardness of being naked around her, even though the Guoke people didn't seem to care about such things.

Weili, like everyone else on this planet, appeared physically flawless, her skin smooth and pale, as though untouched by the passage of time. But there was something deeper about her, something I couldn't quite put into words. Even in her silence, there was intelligence, some knowledge she held about me and the situation we were in.

"That's because our planet's gravity is stronger than Earth's," Norton explained. "But don't worry, I'll fix that."

Norton began manipulating something on a floating panel above the table. Suddenly, my body felt lighter, and the oppressive weight I had been carrying since I arrived lifted.

As he worked, my thoughts kept returning to Weili. She had been with me when they brought me here, witnessing everything. She knew the scientific goals they had set for me, but there was more to her than just the cold logic of these experiments. She hadn't pushed me or made me feel like a mere subject; instead, she seemed to be... watching over me. It was a strange feeling, knowing that the person beside you held such knowledge about your future, yet there was a sense of calm whenever she was around.

"We use the Global Public Movement Network for this," Norton explained, breaking my thoughts. "That's how we moved you from the ship to here in an instant. It's a system that allows for teleportation anywhere on the planet."

"Teleportation?" I echoed, trying to grasp the enormity of what they were telling me.

Norton smiled as he continued. "Yes, it's all based on altering the space around an object. We use something called an artificial field generator, which manipulates space itself. It reduces your mass to almost nothing, allowing you to move at incredible speeds."

I stared at him, struggling to comprehend. "And this system can work on any object or person?"

"On anything, as long as the calculations are correct," he confirmed. "You were just transported 10,000 kilometers in less than a second. No ships, no vehicles. Just the Global Public Movement Network."

I blinked, trying to wrap my mind around it. "And this network… it can move people anywhere? Instantly?"

Weili, sitting quietly beside me, finally spoke. "It's how we get around here," she said softly. "There are no cars, no planes—just the network. It makes life much easier."

Her voice was calm and smooth, as though the concept of teleportation was as simple as taking a walk. I couldn't help but glance at her, wondering how much more she knew about me, about the experiments to come.

Afterward, Norton adjusted the control panel again, and I felt my body grow even lighter. Weili remained by my side the whole time, her quiet presence a constant reminder that, despite everything that had happened, I wasn't alone in this strange new world. Weili's eyes met mine briefly, and for the first time, I realized that this journey would be as much about her as it was about me.

Chapter 8: The Fascinating People of Guoke Planet

One day, while sitting on a virtual sofa at Norton's place, I started to feel hungry. "Hey, I'm getting a bit hungry. What do you guys usually eat here?" I asked.

Norton replied, "Ah, we forgot about that. You Earthlings eat differently from us."

"Really? How do you eat then?" I asked, curiously.

"Our bodies also require energy from food, but we have the global movement network," Norton explained. "When we need energy, we request the network to instantly transport food directly into our bodies. It's usually a liquid that's almost entirely absorbed by our system."

"Liquid food? Do you transport it with bottles into your stomach? How do you digest the bottles?" I joked.

Sudair, who was sitting nearby, laughed. "There's no need for bottles. We don't even have stomachs or intestines like you. Our bodies are very different. From our mouths to our lower bodies, there's just a simple cavity. The food is highly processed and instantly absorbed by our systems. We've outsourced most of our body functions—breathing, digestion, excretion—to external systems via the global movement network. The simpler the body, the more efficient it is, and we've designed ours to be as simple and reliable as possible. It makes us healthier and less prone to disease."

As they spoke, I realized how advanced they were. Norton raised his hand and with a simple wave near his ear, a delicate bottle and metal scissors appeared on the table in front of us.

The bottle was shaped like a penguin, with a sleek silver-white finish that looked metallic. A long spout jutted out like a penguin's beak. Norton snipped the tip off with the scissors and handed me the bottle.

I took a sip. The liquid inside had a floral scent, slightly sweet and refreshing. I drank it all, and instantly, my hunger disappeared. Norton waved his hand again, and both the bottle and the scissors vanished.

"How did you make that bottle appear with just a wave near your ear? Is there some sort of switch there?" I asked, still amazed.

Norton smiled. "Our brains are linked to the global public information network through artificial field scanning. The wave near the ear is just a confirmation gesture. We could set other gestures like shaking our heads, waving, or even stomping our feet. But most of us choose simple, practical gestures to avoid misunderstandings. When our bodies need energy, the network automatically transports it. We've outsourced most of our bodily functions, so we don't have to worry about them."

Laughing, I teased them, "So, without your global movement network, you'd be helpless. What about on the 'Qutu 300' spaceship? You can't use the network there, can you?"

Sudair responded with a chuckle, "Even on 'Qutu 300,' we can access a localized version of the movement network. You just can't see it. And in extreme cases, we can still eat food with our mouths and drink liquids, although our bodies aren't really equipped for it anymore. Our digestive systems have long since evolved into something simpler. If we had to eat like you Earthlings, we could manage, but it wouldn't be easy."

I marveled at their lifestyle and how intertwined it was with their technology. They didn't even need physical digestion anymore.

While we were chatting, my curiosity got the better of me, and I asked, "If your brains are connected to your public information network, like built-in bio-computers, why do you still use virtual screen computers, like the ones I saw on the 'Qutu 300' spaceship?"

Norton explained, "Although our bio-computers are powerful, they aren't as stable or secure as external computers for certain tasks, especially those that require precision, like operating a spaceship. In those cases, we rely on external computers for safety and accuracy."

"Oh, I see. So, there's still structure and order on Guoke Planet. Even with all your advanced technology, you can't just do whatever you want," I replied thoughtfully.

At that moment, I thought of something else. "By the way, Norton, where's your family?"

Norton seemed a bit surprised. "My family?"

"Yeah, your parents, your wife—do you have kids?"

"Oh, I don't have any of those," Norton answered simply.

I turned to Sudair and asked the same. "And you?"

"Just me," Sudair replied, a bit amused.

Then I looked at Weili, who had been quiet but listening intently. "And you, Weili? Do you have parents, siblings?" I hesitated to ask about children, as she looked so young, like a little girl from our elementary schools on Earth.

Weili shook her head, "No, it's just me too."

Shocked, I exclaimed, "You're all alone? No parents, no siblings? That's so sad!"

Sudair laughed dismissively, "Sad? Why would we be sad? On Guoke, we are all immortal. There is no birth or death. So, we have no parents or children, no siblings either. Each of us is our own family."

"Immortal?" I was taken aback, unsure whether to believe them. "You mean you live forever?"

Norton nodded. "Yes, many years ago, we achieved immortality on Guoke. There are no old people, no children. We've moved beyond those cycles of life."

I tried to grasp the idea of living forever. It sounded like something out of an Earthling's dream, but here, it was reality. "But doesn't that make your lives lonely, having no family?"

Weili smiled. "We have pets, and we can communicate with them. Some of us even talk to other animals."

"You can talk to animals?" I asked, amazed.

Norton explained, "Yes, we have ways of translating our thoughts into a language they understand, and through our artificial field scanning, we can send those messages to their brains. Likewise, we can interpret their thoughts.

But you, as an Earthling, might find it hard to comprehend."

I was about to ask more questions when I blurted out, "Do you have relationships? Like, romantic partners?"

Sudair nodded. "Yes, we do. But unlike on Earth, we don't live together or form permanent bonds. Relationships here are temporary, and there's no legal binding."

I was fascinated by how different their lives were, but I couldn't help but wonder how they felt about it all. As we continued talking, I began to see how vastly different Guoke Planet was from anything I could have imagined, yet how seamlessly they had integrated advanced technology into every part of their lives.

Later that day, important guests started arriving at Norton's house, and I noticed something peculiar — some of them appeared out of thin air, while others seemed to materialize slowly from a misty cloud. When I asked Sudair about it, he explained that the ones who appeared instantly were real people using the global movement network, while the misty figures were virtual avatars, just as real as they needed to be for a conversation, but not physically present.

Guoke Planet's technology was beyond anything I had ever imagined, and their society reflected it in every way. As I sat there on the virtual sofa, surrounded by these fascinating people, I realized I had a lot to learn about this strange, wonderful world.

Chapter 9: Why the Guoke People Abduct Earthlings

Sitting on Norton's virtual sofa, I decided to steer the conversation to something less disquieting. "Have you seen Earth women? Do you think they're attractive?"

Norton smiled knowingly. "We've abducted Earthlings many times. I've been to your planet on several occasions, so I'm quite familiar with your people. We regularly abduct not only Earthlings but also beings from many distant planets across the universe. But compared to females from other planets, Earth women aren't particularly remarkable in terms of beauty."

I frowned, puzzled. "Then why abduct Earthlings at all?"

Norton leaned back, his tone becoming more serious. "It's not about looks. We abduct beings not because they're beautiful. When we capture someone, especially from Earth, we use our field scanning technology to extract their thoughts, memories, sensations, movements, and physiological activities into digital form. With that data, we can create an exact replica of the person—identical in every way, down to the smallest detail. We can even delete part or all their consciousness and replace it with a Guoke mind."

Sudair added, "Once we've scanned a being, we can manufacture countless replicas in a short time, ensuring that any Guoke citizen can live in one of these bodies. We abduct beings from all over the universe, not just Earth, and invest huge resources into adapting them to our planet's environment."

"But why go to such lengths to kidnap us?" I asked.

Norton smirked. "What we value is information. In the universe, there are three essentials for life: material resources, energy, and information. On Guoke, material and energy are free, so information is the only valuable currency. Abducting Earthlings and other alien species give us access to unique experiences, which we can monetize. For example, we abduct an Earth man like you, and we make him engage in various activities with females from our system—often sexual in nature. Every movement, every reaction, every thought is digitally recorded."

I was taken aback. "What do you do with all that data?"

Norton shrugged. "We create digital versions of you and sell them. Guoke women can buy a package called 'Living with an Earth Man,' where they can interact with a holographic version of you, just as if you were real. They can chat, live together, and even engage in virtual sex. We also have a more advanced product called 'tangible companions,' where we use a material called 'information mud.' This material, activated by your data, forms a physical replica of you that can be touched, talked to, and felt as if it were the real thing."

Sudair chimed in again, grinning. "Thousands of Guoke women can buy the same Earth man, experiencing life with him all at once. It's like your Earth's popular songs, except instead of music, it's a living, breathing human interaction. Earthlings, unfortunately, haven't been all that popular—your data isn't considered high quality."

"Then why abduct me? Why take anyone from Earth if we're considered low-quality?" I asked, growing more frustrated.

Norton's expression grew more thoughtful. "You are different. When you were around seven or eight years old, something very unusual happened to you, didn't it?"

His words jolted my memory. It was something I had never fully understood, but it had stayed with me all these years.

"One afternoon, when I was about seven, I was out alone, herding geese on a sandy field," I began slowly. "Suddenly, I saw several mist-like shapes darting in front of me. One of them rushed toward me, and I felt a strange buzzing in my head. My vision went black, and I collapsed. When I finally regained consciousness, the mist was gone."

I paused, recalling the strange details. "There was no UFO or spaceship. I only remember a flash of red light in the western sky, near the setting sun, blending with the reddish clouds. I thought it was just a natural light, but something about that moment has stayed with me ever since."

Norton nodded. "That wasn't just a coincidence. You were visited by a civilization far more advanced than ours, and they left an imprint on your brain. That's why we abducted you. We believe they implanted something in your mind—something we can extract."

Sudair added, "That civilization might have transferred advanced knowledge, impressions, or abilities into your brain when you were a child. We're here to uncover whatever they left behind."

Weili, who had remained quiet until now, finally spoke. "They've known about this from the start. That's why you're here—not just for casual study, but because they believe your mind holds a key to something much greater."

Feeling the weight of her words, I asked, "And the other Earthlings you've abducted—what happened to them?"

Norton looked indifferent. "Some were sent back. Others... well, they didn't survive the experiments. Some couldn't handle the strain of our tests, or died while engaging in... activities with our females. A few lived out the rest of their lives here, too old or too weak to return. But most were simply... forgotten."

Sudair laughed, his body shaking with amusement. "We're not perfect. Sometimes we get lazy."

Weili, sensing my growing anxiety, reassured me. "Don't worry, you're different. What's in your brain is too valuable to lose. They won't let you die."

As unsettling as that was, I couldn't shake the feeling that this was only the beginning. The Guoke people were playing a much larger game, one that spanned galaxies and civilizations—and I had somehow become a crucial part of it.

Chapter 10: Land-Based and Water-Based Species in the Universe

Sitting on Norton's virtual sofa one day, I found myself immersed in the marvels of the Guoke world. Out of curiosity, I turned to Norton and asked, "Other than Earthlings and Guoke people, are there many other humanoid species in the universe?"

Norton smiled and responded, "Absolutely. The universe is filled with life, and many intelligent species exist. However, their origins and evolutionary paths differ. Some evolved from land-based creatures, like us, and others evolved from water-based lifeforms."

"Water-based?" I leaned forward, intrigued. "That sounds fascinating. Can you tell me more?"

Norton explained, "In the universe, most intelligent species fall into two main categories based on their evolutionary roots: land-based and water-based species. Both categories have unique strengths and weaknesses. Land-based species, like Earthlings and Guoke people, evolved on land. Although early life on Earth began in water, most of your evolution happened on land, so you're classified as a land-based species. Most species in the universe, like us, fall into this category."

"Even birds and flying creatures are considered land-based," he added. "Despite their ability to fly, their evolutionary process took place mostly on land."

He paused, his expression thoughtful. "But water-based species are something entirely different. These species evolved in aquatic environments, and their bodies reflect that. Guoke people have a particular fascination with water-based species because their physical characteristics are incredibly unique."

I couldn't help but ask, "So how do Earthlings rank among all these different species? Are our bodies considered advanced?"

Weili, who had been listening quietly, jumped in with a teasing grin. "Not really. Your bodies are quite… basic."

Sudair laughed as well, adding, "Honestly, Earthlings have some of the least impressive physical traits in the universe."

I was surprised. "Really? Why is that?"

Norton explained, "It's because of the way you evolved. As land-based species, both Earthlings and Guoke people share similar evolutionary paths. Natural selection favored certain physical traits— four limbs, a head to navigate, and bipedal movement for tool use. Over time, these traits optimized survival in a land environment."

He waved his hand, and a 3D hologram appeared, displaying various land-based species from different planets. While they each had their own distinct features, their general body structure was surprisingly like humans.

"Most land-based species look quite alike," Norton continued, "because evolution across the universe tends to follow the same path. Walking on two legs, using hands for tools—these are efficient ways to survive. That's why you and we look so similar, even though we come from different planets."

"What about water-based species?" I asked, curious about how they differed.

Norton's face lit up with excitement. "Water-based species are extraordinary. Their evolution happened in a completely different environment, which gave them abilities and physical attributes that land-based beings can't even imagine. They've been perfecting their forms for billions of years, and some of their traits are so highly specialized that they don't need tools or technology like we do."

He elaborated, "For instance, many water-based species have evolved the ability to split their bodies into smaller parts while retaining full control over each piece. This allows them to parasitize larger land-based creatures, controlling and enhancing their hosts while living inside them. Over time, they've become experts at this, developing symbiotic relationships that land-based creatures could never achieve."

Sudair joined in, "These water-based beings often provide incredible pleasure to their hosts, far beyond what land-based beings can experience. The sensation is so intense that most hosts don't want to escape, even though the parasitic relationship can be dangerous."

I tried to wrap my head around it. "So, they share their bodies with other beings?"

"Yes," Norton said. "It's a form of biological symbiosis. If you experience regular intimacy with another being, we might rate that as a 1 on a scale of pleasure. When a water-based species shares their body with you, the pleasure can reach a 5. If they're large enough to engulf you entirely, that can go up to a 10. It's a completely different level of experience, but it comes with risks—fear and pain can also intensify."

I shuddered at the thought. These creatures had evolved in ways that made them almost incomprehensible to someone like me, used to a land-based existence.

"In the Guoke system," Norton continued, "we have many water-based species that were brought here from other planets. They're powerful, intelligent, and in some cases, terrifying. Some of them can swallow smaller beings whole, absorbing them into their bodies and making it nearly impossible for the absorbed being to escape."

Weili added softly, "Smaller water-based creatures are sneakier. They can invade your body before you even realize what's happening, controlling you from the inside."

These descriptions gave me a chill. It was hard to believe that such beings could exist, let alone coexist with a species like the Guoke people.

Norton then said, "The most powerful water-based species can be both terrifying and awe-inspiring. They have abilities that make them nearly impossible to resist once they've set their sights on you."

He paused, reflecting for a moment. "But as amazing as water-based species are, they still face challenges. They can't use tools or technology the way we do, and that limits their development. In many cases, their entire evolution focuses on perfecting their bodies, but not their societies. So, while they might have the upper hand in physical abilities, land-based species like us often surpass them in technological advancement."

The more I learned, the more I realized just how vast and diverse the universe really was. The Guoke people had mastered the art of manipulating their bodies and their environment, but they weren't the only species out there with unique strengths. The water-based beings they admired had evolved in ways that were equally impressive, offering a glimpse of the endless possibilities of life beyond Earth.

Chapter 11: The Strange Sexual Behaviors of the Guoke People

Norton once explained to me the reasons behind the strange sexual behaviors of the Guoke people, providing insight into their society's unique views on sex.

"On Earth," Norton began, "sex serves two main purposes: reproduction and the maintenance of a family, as well as providing pleasure for yourself and your partner. Your relationships are not just about sexual attraction but also about co-managing a life together. Financial stability and material wealth are key to nurturing a family and raising the next generation. In fact, material wealth plays such a significant role that men and women often exchange gifts or wealth to bring joy and maintain their connection."

He paused, looking at me intently. "But sex on Earth is also influenced by laws, moral codes, cultural traditions, religion, and social expectations. There's love between men and women, there's care, support, and the partnership of building a family together. In our society, things are much simpler — sex is purely about pleasure, sensation, and experience. There's no love, no romance, and certainly no need to care for children or manage resources."

I was stunned by his words. "But why is it so different for you?"

"Material resources mean nothing to us," Norton continued. "We don't have children or the concept of family like you do. We have no death, no illness, no concern for safety, health, or longevity. There's no need to earn a living, no need to form partnerships or care for offspring. Since our lives are guaranteed to be eternal and healthy, we don't have those additional layers that Earthlings attach to relationships."

He leaned back in his seat. "We also don't have constraints of laws or moral codes. Sex often involves violence here—sometimes extreme violence. That's why many of us prefer virtual sexual experiences, where we can stop at any moment and avoid the danger of physical harm."

Norton's explanation made me think. "So, your lives revolve around the search for pleasure, specifically through sexual experience?"

"Yes," he confirmed. "While you Earthlings pursue wealth and power, our lives are centered on pleasure and experience. And of all experiences, sex is the most pleasurable. That's why our people are so focused on it — it's not about love or companionship, but about pure sensation."

His words reminded me of something Sudair had mentioned earlier, about how the Guoke people see no difference between sex with a human or with an animal. Norton's final comment solidified that thought.

"In a way," Norton added, "sex between an Earthling and a Guoke person is not much different from sex with an animal. Guoke people don't have emotions tied to love. We are driven by the pursuit of experience."

As if reading my discomfort, Norton shifted the topic slightly to discuss the sexual behaviors of parasitic species on their planet.

"One of the most extreme examples is the relationship between parasitic beings and their hosts," Norton explained. "Unlike Earth, where parasites feed off the host's body for sustenance, on Guoke, material resources and food are irrelevant. The most intense battles we have are not for wealth, food, or power, but for control of each other's bodies—through parasitic invasion."

I was shocked by this revelation. "How does that work? Are these parasites violent?"

"Parasitic behavior here is far more advanced and complex than anything on Earth," Norton said. "Our technology has allowed us to enhance these traits. Unlike on Earth, where romantic love is held in high regard, our society has evolved into one where parasitic control of another's body is a form of domination. It's no longer about affection—our relationships have become invasive, often violent, and, by Earth's standards, incredibly bizarre."

He continued, "Parasites here don't destroy their hosts. Instead, they use the host's body for their own pleasure, often turning them into sexual slaves. This behavior is deeply rooted in the ancient survival instincts of our species. Even with our technology, these primal behaviors have adapted and evolved, transforming into highly advanced, yet disturbingly aggressive forms of sexual control."

Norton's words left me with an unsettling feeling. The picture he painted was of a society where violence, control, and domination had taken the place of love, affection, and partnership. He described a world where intimacy was transactional, devoid of emotion, and driven solely by the pursuit of sensory pleasure.

He concluded by saying, "On Earth, sex is tied to love and affection. In Guoke, it's more about power, control, and sometimes even violence. It's a game of dominance, not of connection. That's why our parasitic relationships are so prevalent and why our sexual behaviors seem strange to outsiders."

I was left with more questions than answers. In the Guoke world, the boundaries of intimacy had stretched far beyond anything I could have imagined, leaving me with a lingering sense of unease about the true nature of their relationships.

Chapter 12: Norton's Explanation of the Origin of All Life in the Universe

One day, I asked Norton, "Where do we Earthlings come from? Many people on Earth say we were created by God. I don't really believe that, but given your advanced technology, I'm inclined to believe that maybe you created us. Have you ever seeded life on other planets or placed your people among other species?"

Norton responded, "While we now possess the technology to create life, including our own bodies, it wasn't always like this. You Earthlings, we Guoke people, and the other intelligent species across the universe—most of us didn't originate from external seeding or creation by any superior being. Life on most planets with intelligent species evolved naturally, from simpler forms to more complex organisms."

He paused for a moment, then added, "You humans weren't created by God or any higher deity. That idea of God is simply a construct, a set of information invented by your species. Like all life, you evolved, and over time, your species developed those beliefs as a way to explain existence."

Norton's words struck me deeply. I had never heard such a clear rejection of creation myths from a being so advanced.

"We now have the ability to manufacture life, to create anything from simple organisms to advanced beings," Norton continued. "But this capability is a result of technological advancement over time.

Your Earth, and all its life, began more than a billion years ago with a lightning strike."

"A lightning strike?" I asked curiously.

"Yes," Norton confirmed. "About a billion years ago, a lightning bolt struck the nitrogen in Earth's atmosphere, creating complex molecules. These molecules fell into water and formed amino acids and proteins. From there, the earliest self-replicating virus-like organisms appeared. Over billions of years, these primitive life forms evolved into more complex creatures."

Norton explained that every advanced life form in the universe is a survivor of a long battle with viruses. "Life's progress is constantly hindered by waves of viral annihilation. Most life fails to survive, and those that do often regress to simpler forms to avoid extinction. The journey from simple organisms to complex beings capable of consciousness is incredibly rare in the universe. Less than one in a billion planets with life succeed in evolving to intelligent species."

Earth's evolutionary history, according to Norton, wasn't far off from what scientists believed, though he offered a more nuanced view. "Your scientists think humans evolved from apes, apes from reptiles, and reptiles from aquatic life. But the story is more complicated than that. Early life didn't emerge from the oceans. It began in small ponds and freshwater lakes on land, where conditions were better suited for the development of the first self-replicating organisms. The oceans were too harsh— salty, mineral-rich, and turbulent. Life later migrated to the seas, not the other way around."

Norton explained how certain freshwater creatures adapted to the oceans over billions of years, while some aquatic creatures, in extreme circumstances, adapted to life on land. He talked about how Earth's creatures gradually evolved to survive in drier environments.

"Think of your Earth's blackfish," Norton said. "It can survive out of water for days. It evolved into mudfish, then into creatures like eel, which can survive months without water. Eventually, this evolved into species like snakes, which can survive entirely on land."

He went on to describe the progression of life on Earth. "The evolution of animals, from creatures that could live in dry land, led to the emergence of species like rabbits, then to primates, and finally to you humans. You can even see traces of this evolutionary journey in your own bodies, like the tail present in human embryos."

Norton's explanation didn't stop at Earth. He began discussing the evolution of awareness and intelligence in the universe. "As organisms evolve, they develop more complex methods of controlling their bodies, which leads to the evolution of consciousness. Early life had simple reflexes — moving towards food, moving away from danger. Over time, as organisms developed more senses, their control systems became more sophisticated, leading to the formation of what you call 'awareness' or 'consciousness.'"

Norton then added, "Even now, you and I are just complex beings made up of electronic signals and particles. Our thoughts are merely the product of electrical charges and ions moving through our brains, something that took billions of years to develop."

But as life evolved, not all took the same path. "Some species evolved towards simplicity instead of complexity," he said. "Viruses, for instance, simplified themselves to the most basic survival forms, which makes them so effective. Sometimes, simpler is better for survival."

When I asked if they had ever introduced life on other planets, Norton acknowledged that Guoke people had tried. "We've placed life forms and even designed intelligent beings on other planets. But it's difficult to simulate the evolutionary journey that natural life takes. Life that evolves naturally forms a deep bond with its environment through constant adaptation. It's hard for us to create that artificially."

Norton explained that while they had designed and seeded some planets with life, the results weren't ideal. "Even though we've used supercomputers to simulate billions of years of evolution and used time-manipulating 'temporal refrigerators' to model their survival, many of these artificially placed beings fail to thrive on new planets. It's because they lack the deep connection with the environment that natural evolution creates."

He described Earth as an example of the randomness of evolution. "Your planet has a unique history, shaped by viruses and environmental conditions over billions of years. For example, your aversion to industrial noise is because your species has adapted to the sounds of nature over millions of years. The birdsong in the forests is familiar to your genes, while the noise of factories is something your body hasn't had time to adjust to."

Norton explained that while Guoke people had advanced capabilities to manipulate life and bodies, they had shifted their focus from creating new life forms to something more direct. "Rather than placing beings on other planets, we now prefer to kidnap them, as we did with you. It's more beneficial for us to study and extract information from other species than to place our own and hope they survive."

With that, I realized how different their philosophy was. While they had the capability to shape life and influence evolution, they now saw more value in observing, experimenting, and even abducting other species from across the galaxy. Their interest in Earth and other planets wasn't about dominance or creation — it was about discovery and exploitation.

"We find it easier to study and benefit from the lives of beings who have already adapted to their environment," Norton said. "That's why we're here, and that's why you're here now."

Chapter 13: Are There Many Planets with Intelligent Life in the Universe?

One day, I asked Norton, "Just how big is the universe? And how many kinds of aliens are out there?"

Norton replied, "The universe, as we once thought, seemed like an infinite space with a limited number of stars and planets concentrated at the center. For a long time, our understanding reflected this view, and many advanced civilizations shared the same concept. But as our scientific observation tools improved, we discovered something astonishing: new planets located trillions of light years away. This shattered our previously unwavering view of the universe."

He paused, his expression serious. "We now know that the universe is layered, like the structure of an onion. It's infinite in size, and we can't yet determine whether the number of planets is infinite. Our ability to answer that question depends on the limits of our observational capabilities. But through other avenues, we've concluded that the number of planets is indeed unending."

Norton explained that while the universe is filled with countless planets, the vast majority are barren, without life. "Of the planets that do harbor life, only a small fraction have intelligent species like those on Earth. The rough estimate is that for each one intelligent species, there are tens of thousands of planets with only primitive lifeforms still in their early stages of evolution. As for highly advanced planets like Guoke, which can build light-speed crafts and travel freely across the cosmos, those are far rarer, around one in a billion."

He added, "And yes, there are even civilizations more advanced than ours."

I was stunned. "More advanced than you? But you seem so advanced already," I said.

Norton smiled faintly. "Oh, there are indeed many civilizations far beyond ours. These civilizations have mastered technologies that allow them to explore the universe at a level we can only imagine. When a species develops the ability to travel at the speed of light, it becomes a hallmark of a developed civilization. The ability to traverse galaxies quickly is what separates the advanced from the primitive."

He continued, "So, we categorize intelligent planets in two main groups. First, there are those that have deciphered the core principles of the universe — time, space, force, mass, charge, and energy. These planets can build light-speed crafts and conduct large-scale interstellar travel. The second group consists of planets like yours, which are still bound by slower methods of travel and haven't yet broken the barriers of advanced physics."

Norton outlined how planets could be further classified by their technological age. "A planet that invents light-speed technology and develops for over a thousand years falls into what we call a 'Millennium-Level Civilization,' like Guoke. Planets that have advanced for tens of thousands of years become 'Ten-Thousand-Year Civilizations,' and those that have evolved for millions or even billions of years fall into the rarest category."

I was curious, so I asked, "How do you measure advancement?"

Norton explained, "We measure a civilization's development by its level of virtualization. The more virtual a society is, the more advanced it is. In the most advanced civilizations, nearly everything is virtual—information processing, bodies, buildings, transportation, and even industrial manufacturing. Planets with a virtualization rate close to 100% are considered extremely advanced. If the rate is around 50%, they're still considered advanced, but anything below that is less so. From our data, most planets with life are even less developed than Earth."

Sudair interjected, "There's an unspoken rule in the universe: planets that are less advanced and can't conduct interstellar travel are usually monitored and protected by more advanced planets. This is partly to prevent overly aggressive interference from other powerful civilizations and to ensure that internal conflicts, especially nuclear wars, don't destroy the planet entirely. The intervention is subtle—most often, the minds of key figures are remotely influenced, rather than through direct involvement."

Norton added, "For instance, during World War II on your planet, Germany had the technical know-how to develop nuclear weapons, but extraterrestrial intervention prevented their success. Your Earth is still considered a primitive planet by universal standards, as you haven't developed light-speed travel, and you're bound by momentum conservation principles in your physics. Our light-speed crafts are also governed by momentum conservation, but we operate on a more complex system, where momentum is a function of mass multiplied by vector light-speed minus the velocity of the object."

I was struggling to grasp the complexities of their science, so Norton simplified it for me. "There are much more advanced civilizations that have developed ships that can bypass the limitations of both time and space. Their technology eliminates accidents altogether."

Intrigued, I asked, "What else do these super-advanced civilizations do?"

Norton revealed something that shook me to the core. "These ancient civilizations, which have existed for millions or even billions of years, are incredibly advanced, and their level of mathematical understanding is so far beyond ours it's terrifying. They've developed technologies like liquid metals that can penetrate a human body and alter or delete consciousness. For example, we could inject a liquid metal into an Earthling, completely erasing their mind and replacing it with the mind of a Guoke person. To everyone else, that Earthling would still look the same, but they'd be, for all intents and purposes, dead."

He added, "These higher civilizations use a set of mathematical codes to control such technology. Even if they gave us their simplest codes, it would take us centuries to understand them. Meanwhile, they can effortlessly decode any of our most complex formulas."

Norton's explanation of the power of mathematics seemed beyond belief. "For them," he said, "mathematics is the battlefield. Unlike your planet, where you wage wars with weapons and armies, they engage in silent contests of mathematical prowess. Their superiority lies in their ability to predict and control everything, from viruses to the flow of information in the universe. They can calculate the spread of future pandemics before they even happen."

Finally, Norton concluded, "The civilizations that have advanced for billions of years hold unimaginable power. They can't be reasoned with or challenged. For us, their presence is akin to the appearance of gods."

Sudair, chuckling awkwardly, added, "We can freely travel around the universe and abduct people from less advanced planets. If we abduct someone from a highly advanced planet, we make sure to send them back because we don't want to provoke any retaliation. But with more primitive worlds like yours, we sometimes don't bother. We let nature take its course," he said with an awkward laugh.

Chapter 14: The Religion of Guoke Planet

One day, while talking with Norton, Sudair, and Weili, I asked about religion.

I said, "Religion plays a significant role on Earth, with major religions like Christianity, Buddhism, and Islam shaping our society. So, does the universe have any gods—an almighty being, a Buddha, or Allah? If they exist, where are they? Does Guoke Planet have religion? If so, what kind of influence does it have on you?"

Sudair was quick to respond, "There are no gods, Buddhas, or divine beings in the universe. These are concepts your Earth people invented. We don't have religion on Guoke Planet."

Norton added, "There was a time, in the early days of our technological development, when we did have religion. However, as our society advanced, religion was marginalized and has nearly vanished. Today, it's rarely mentioned and only exists in our history and memories."

Norton continued his explanation:

"Science and religion are both ways of understanding the world, but they originate from different places. Science stems from human curiosity and rationality, while religion is born from fear and instinct. Early societies, both on Earth and on Guoke Planet, were primitive. People were afraid of the unknown—wild beasts, lightning, floods, disease, and even death. These fears led them to create imaginary beings—gods and spirits—to protect them and provide comfort. This is how religion began.

In those early, underdeveloped times, people lacked understanding of the natural world. So, they feared everything, and religion thrived while science was weak. At the dawn of human civilization, science and religion were not separated. As knowledge grew, the two diverged, with science and religion developing in opposite directions.

As humans gained more understanding, science grew stronger, expanding its reach and depth. Meanwhile, religion's power dwindled. The more science explained the world, the more religion's simplistic and sometimes absurd explanations became evident. Eventually, religious explanations of the universe, life, and society started to seem childish, while science, with its logic, precision, and ability to quantify the world, gained more credibility.

Guoke Planet's people have uncovered the core secrets of the universe—those hidden within space itself. We now fully comprehend the nature of space, time, and energy. With that knowledge, our reverence for the mysteries of the cosmos has disappeared. The fear and uncertainty that once gave rise to religion no longer exist here.

The disappearance of death also played a significant role. We have conquered death through technology, giving us eternal life. Without the fear of death, there is no need for religion. This is why religion has faded away on our planet, and we believe this is the trend for all advanced civilizations in the universe.

On highly advanced planets like ours, people can create their own bodies, live forever, and even replace their physical form with virtual bodies made of light. We can cure any disease instantly and provide for everyone's needs with minimal effort. With artificial intelligence handling most of our labor, both physical and mental, and resources in abundance, there's no need for wars or competition over material wealth. Here, we don't need morality, laws, or religion to suppress human desires — we can satisfy them through science.

On Earth, you still need morality, laws, and religion to control both good and evil impulses, especially when resources are limited. For example, on Earth, a man with inappropriate desires for a young girl must be restrained by laws, morals, or religious teachings. But here, we have developed highly realistic virtual experiences to fulfill such desires without harm. These experiences are so realistic that even our most advanced senses cannot distinguish them from reality.

You see, on Earth, you use morality and religion to restrain desires because you can't satisfy everyone's needs. When that fails, you turn to religion for help. But here on Guoke Planet, we use science to fulfill desires, whether noble or wicked. With no need to restrain such impulses, religion has lost its relevance.

The foundation of religion — fear — and its function — to suppress desires — have disappeared here. That's why religion has become irrelevant in our society."

Norton paused and then added, "In Earth's history, religion has wielded immense power for centuries, shaping your cultures and beliefs. But even on Earth, its influence is waning. Religious leaders no longer hold the same power they once did, and people no longer revere them as much. Instead, people now admire and look up to scientists, seeing them as the new visionaries who can unlock the mysteries of the universe.

The future of Earth will be much like our own. As science advances, religion will continue to fade, replaced by the wonders of scientific discovery. Eventually, people will no longer believe in the simple, intuitive explanations offered by religion, as science will have revealed all the answers to the universe's deepest mysteries."

Sudair chimed in, "Some people believe that highly advanced planets maintain strong religious systems, controlling the minds of their inhabitants through faith. But from our exploration of the universe, we've found that the more advanced a civilization is, the weaker religion's grip becomes. Science and religion are not complementary — they are fundamentally at odds with each other."

Chapter 15: First Examination and Human Experiments

One day, Norton, Sudair, and Weili led me into a room where two other figures, likely robots, were present. In the center of the room was a narrow bed, just large enough for one person, covered in a white sheet—or something resembling it, possibly a virtual construct. The head of the bed was elevated quite high.

Norton spoke solemnly, "We're going to examine your body now. Trust our technology; it won't cause you any pain or discomfort. Please lie down on the bed."

Though I obeyed, laying on the bed, I was filled with fear, imagining my body being dissected, cut open with sharp blades, and enduring unbearable pain. The room suddenly plunged into darkness, and I felt a strange sensation—like I was floating above myself, watching from a distance as my body lay on the bed. Everything looked vivid, but the colors seemed off. Was this some sort of visual information service from their global public information network?

At the head and foot of the bed, two figures stood. One of them used a thin, square blade to cut a small opening in my throat and gently brushed the area, like using a feather. Strangely, I felt no pain — just a ticklish, tingling sensation. The global information network's assistant, Kewen, translated their conversation for me, explaining that my throat had some issues and that I would suffer from a throat condition for the rest of my life.

Sure enough, in my twenties, I developed chronic throat inflammation, a condition that continues to plague me. Despite numerous treatments and wasted money, I've never found relief.

When the light returned, I felt my floating self merge back with my body. Relieved that there was no physical pain, I touched my throat, feeling normal. I sat up as Norton approached and asked me something, which Kewen translated: "Do you feel anything near your abdomen or thighs?"

"Yes, it felt like a cold snake slithering through there," I replied.

"Where did it go?" Norton asked, tilting his head in thought. He didn't wait for my answer and walked away. A wave of fear washed over me as I imagined that a snake might have entered my body. The thought filled me with nausea, and my earlier relief vanished.

This was just the first of many examinations and experiments. In some, I felt not only snakes but also tubes and leech-like creatures invading my body. One time, I felt as if I had been reduced to a skeleton, lying in the open under the scorching sun of a desert. My body was so dry, and I felt extreme heat.

"Who is this?" I asked, confused.

"That's you!" Kewen's voice answered.

"How can this be me?" I thought, but no further answers came. It was a strange nightmare, but I soon woke up, relieved that the experiment had ended.

Some experiments were more invasive and exhausting, particularly when I felt massive, fleshy tubes entering through my body. One tube was so thick it felt like it was the size of my arm, moving forcefully inside me. After such sessions, I would collapse into a deep, sweat-soaked sleep, waking utterly drained.

During one simulation, I felt as though I had fallen from the sky, landing on a bed of sharp, metallic needles that pierced my abdomen. The sudden, excruciating pain caused me to black out. Norton later explained that it was all a simulation, designed to test how many needles I could endure before reaching a fatal threshold. The purpose was to prepare me for potential interactions with the Guoke women, who had internal flesh tubes that might pierce through my abdomen during sexual contact.

His explanation filled me with a deep fear of their women.

Sometimes during these experiments, I would fall into a deep sleep, my legs stretched out uncomfortably, leaving me sore upon waking. It seemed they noticed my discomfort, as they began placing cushions beneath my knees during these sessions. Over time, I learned to adjust my body into more comfortable positions before drifting off to sleep, minimizing discomfort afterward.

Later, I underwent numerous hallucinatory experiments.

Norton once told me, "We're going to conduct a hallucinatory experiment on you, making you experience various illusions."

His words filled me with dread, fearing it might be like drug addiction. Norton reassured me, saying, "It's simply a way to create vivid hallucinations, without any pain or harm to your body. There's no risk of addiction, and the experiences can even be quite pleasant."

He explained that on Guoke Planet, such hallucinations were common, both voluntarily and involuntarily, much like how people on Earth eat or smoke. Despite his assurances, I couldn't shake my fear. But I trusted their advanced technology, and so I lay on the bed, waiting for them to inject me or administer some drug.

However, instead of needles or pills, I quickly slipped into a hallucinatory state.

I found myself inside a small container, surrounded by fleshy tubes resembling pig intestines. The air was thick with a foul stench. I wished the space would expand, and to my surprise, it did. The container grew enormous, with pig intestines draped across the sky and ground. I seemed to hover in the air, no longer standing on the intestines. When I looked at myself, I saw only a vague glow, my body invisible.

I wondered if these intestines would transform into worms, and they did — giant, wriggling maggots covering every surface. I could even see their detailed, squirming bodies. It soon became clear that my thoughts controlled the hallucinations. I imagined the worms turning into women's legs— specifically, Earth women's legs.

Instantly, an overwhelming scene appeared: the sky and ground filled with smooth, feminine legs, radiating an intoxicating fragrance. It all felt incredibly real and tempting, except for the fact that some of these women had flesh tubes emerging from their bodies, wrapping around my neck and arms. These, clearly, were not Earth women but Guoke women.

The visions continued to shift and change, eventually becoming worms, snakes, and octopus-like creatures, and later transforming into soft hands, vibrant flowers, and bizarre, pulsating streets and buildings. Everything changed continuously, yet the scenes maintained a strange order and symmetry.

These hallucinations, unlike those caused by drugs or toxins, were vivid and coherent, complete with smells, colors, and emotions. Kewen explained that this was how the global information network created hallucinations—by directly interfacing with my brain. It was a highly efficient and cost-effective method compared to drug-induced hallucinations, which were more common among Guoke's parasitic women.

The illusions caused by drugs distorted one's perception of familiar objects, warping colors, shapes, and movements. But the hallucinations created by the global information network were far more elaborate, taking me into entirely new, strange worlds with unfamiliar people and settings. The stories and experiences were consistent and captivating.

On Guoke Planet, hallucinatory experiences were often paired with dream manipulation to control others, especially in relationships. This practice was entirely accepted on their planet.

Unlike drug-induced hallucinations on Earth, which could cause harm or even death, the global information network's method left no lasting damage. Their hallucinatory experiments were sophisticated, allowing them to manipulate one's perceptions without any physical side effects.

Chapter 16: The Indulgence of Guoke People and My Alien Girlfriend

On Guoke Planet, I quickly noticed the uninhibited nature of the people, especially when it came to sexuality. It was not uncommon to witness fully naked individuals, and even couples engaging in sexual activities in public, particularly in dimly lit underwater and subterranean worlds. Their clothing would sometimes appear small, barely visible, or disappear entirely. The skin of Guoke people could also change colors dramatically, becoming radiant and bright, especially in the presence of the opposite sex. The intensity of these changes was striking, with vibrant colors and flashes of light emanating from their bodies.

Once, while walking with Weili, Sudair, and Norton, we came across six Guoke women sitting on the ground. Upon seeing us, they excitedly waved and moved their bodies seductively. As they noticed my tall, unusual Earthling appearance, one by one, their clothing disappeared. Their naked bodies gleamed under the bright light, and I couldn't help but feel the tension in the air as some of the women extended slender, shining tendrils from their lower bodies, resembling skirts made of fine metallic wires.

At one point, a woman even hovered above us, legs apart, with the aid of the Global Movement Network. I could see the vivid details of her anatomy as she floated over my head. My heart pounded with a mix of shock and arousal, though my Earthly upbringing struggled to accept the blatant display. These women were far more direct and provocative than anything I'd experienced before.

"What shameless women," I thought aloud, despite feeling captivated. "On Earth, they would be arrested."

Norton and Sudair laughed at my reaction, while Weili looked unamused. "These women must have used a directed shield," Weili explained. "You saw their true behavior, but Norton and Sudair didn't — they saw only the image the women projected to them, probably because they weren't the intended audience."

I couldn't help but question the lack of morality and self-control I observed. "We on Earth believe that as technology advances, so should morality. How can such a highly developed civilization have such little restraint?"

Norton explained patiently, "We don't uphold the same moral standards you Earthlings do. We believe that technology exists to satisfy human desires, both good and bad. Our society evolved past the need for laws and morality. Instead of suppressing desires, we find ways to indulge them safely. This is why we've developed highly immersive virtual technologies—so individuals can act on their darkest desires without causing harm to others."

Though his explanation made some sense in the context of their society, it still clashed with everything I knew from Earth.

One evening, Sudair suggested that we go out for fun. Norton eagerly agreed and called his girlfriend via the Global Information Network. Soon after, a beautiful woman appeared—her features sharp, her body petite and finely detailed. Her hair, resembling black rubber tubes with glittering strands, hung in two smooth braids. Her clothes—or perhaps the virtual image of clothes—were minimal, revealing much of her soft skin.

Norton's girlfriend was captivating, and I couldn't help but feel embarrassed by my own nakedness as she approached me. "You must be the Earthling, Qian Ge," she said with a bright smile. "You're quite handsome. Can I touch you?"

I hesitated but nodded. She gently touched my hand and then my face, noting how warm my skin felt compared to her own. Her cold but smooth touch was strangely pleasant, though I sensed Weili's irritation.

Not to be outdone, Sudair contacted his own girlfriend, who appeared soon after. She was equally beautiful, though with a more exotic, almost eerie appearance. Her eyes sparkled like diamonds, and her skin transitioned from soft flesh to metallic surfaces around her eyes, adding to her mysterious allure.

I couldn't help but ask Weili about her partner. "Where's your boyfriend?" I asked, trying to be polite.

She turned her head with a proud flick, not answering. Sudair chuckled, "Qian Ge, you are her boyfriend! We promised you a partner when you arrived on Guoke, and that partner is Weili."

Surprised, I looked at Weili. "Really? Weili, am I your boyfriend?"

"You are not my boyfriend," she said disdainfully. "You are my... pet."

Confused, I turned to Sudair, who burst into laughter. "She means you're her plaything, Qian Ge. You're not a real boyfriend, more like a toy."

"Don't worry, Qian Ge," Norton added, "Weili will take good care of you."

Though unsure of what to think, I followed the group as we ventured out into the city. Norton and Sudair walked arm-in-arm with their girlfriends, while I awkwardly followed behind Weili, too nervous to make any physical contact. The city was bustling with virtual lights and grand floating structures that made Earth's cities pale in comparison. Yet, the strangeness of it all — the sight of virtual people, the bizarre floating buildings, the surreal environment — was still overwhelming.

As we walked through different interactive environments, I found myself immersed in a range of strange sensations, from walking through liquid-like substances to being bombarded with virtual beams of light. At one point, Weili and I ended up in an odd experience where we were coated in a transparent gel and rolled down a set of stairs together, causing her to laugh wildly as we bounced and tumbled.

Later, back at Weili's place, the evening took a more intimate turn. Her home was filled with strange decor, including semi-transparent fabrics and exotic plants, giving off a pinkish hue. As I sat down to eat the food she summoned, I realized that my relationship with Weili was about to deepen. After finishing my meal, I approached her, and she began to remove her virtual clothes—though, as I would later learn, they were never real to begin with.

Weili's body was unlike anything I had imagined. Her smooth, hairless skin began to change colors, and from her lower body, several soft, flexible tubes emerged — her real sexual organs. The sight was both terrifying and fascinating, and I couldn't resist the pull of desire, despite my lingering fear.

Our physical intimacy was both familiar and alien. Though her anatomy was strange, the sensations I experienced were intense. Her body responded in ways I never thought possible, leaving me utterly exhausted by the end. But as thrilling as it was, I quickly learned that Weili, like all Guoke women, had far greater physical stamina than I did.

Chapter 17: Strolling in the Clouds with My Alien Girlfriend

After a deep sleep, exhausted from the previous night, I woke up to Weili gently stroking my face. As I opened my eyes, I saw daylight streaming through the room.

"We're going out today," Weili said. "I've talked to Norton and the others, and we've got some time for ourselves."

I quickly realized that on Guoke Planet, where advanced technology takes care of everything, daily life revolves around leisure. There's no work, just endless ways to play. I suggested to Weili that we visit the countryside. She stared at me blankly, not responding, likely unfamiliar with the concept of rural areas.

"We could go somewhere with open fields, with dirt," I explained, hoping she would understand.

Without saying a word, she pressed her hand to her ear, and in an instant, we vanished from her house and reappeared in a vast natural area.

Guoke Planet didn't have cities or rural areas like on Earth, but rather, areas for human habitation and non-habitation. The ground in the human areas was covered in special materials, while in non-habitation zones, the ground was bare. The soil here was a rich red color, possibly from a high iron content. Surrounding us were various plants—tall trees, and strange flowers and grasses of bright, vivid colors. Everything was alive with greens, whites, yellows, and reds, with occasional blue or black flowers adding an air of mystery.

The grass was thick, the plants large and waxy, with no sign of wilting or decay. Small ponds dotted the land, though I saw no familiar Earth creatures like eels or fish. Still, the landscape was serene. The sun shone brightly, yet the air was cool, a strange contrast to the usual warmth of a sunny day.

As we walked among the flowers and trees, we came across a small green hut made entirely of vines. It had doors, windows, and even a staircase, all formed by the natural growth of the plants. It was an incredibly intricate structure, and small insects crawled along the vines.

I embraced Weili as we wandered through the hut, the atmosphere making me feel as if I'd lived this moment before. An overwhelming sense of déjà vu struck me as if I had dreamed of this place before — dreamed of this exact scene, with a woman in my arms.

Unable to resist the urge, I pulled Weili to the ground, and we tumbled among the vines, laughing and rolling together. The moment felt too surreal, too familiar, as if I had longed for this encounter my entire life. Weili didn't resist; in fact, she encouraged it, her virtual clothes disappearing as we engaged in yet another intimate moment.

Afterward, as I held her, her virtual clothing slowly reappeared, the colors of her skin shifting back to pale white. We left the vine hut and walked into the open air again, where I felt a sudden lightness under my feet. Both of us began to rise into the air, floating effortlessly.

"What's happening?" I asked, alarmed at the sudden change.

"This is the Global Movement Network," Weili explained. "It's moving us in tiny increments, so small and fast that it feels like we're floating."

The concept made sense. "Ah, I see! Since the distances and times are so minuscule, we can't perceive the movement, so it feels like we're suspended in mid-air," I said.

Weili smiled. "Exactly! You really are smart."

We drifted effortlessly through the sky, higher and higher, until we entered the clouds. The mist surrounded us, making me feel as if I were walking on air, like Sun Wukong riding on a cloud. The experience was exhilarating, but the clouds obscured our view of the ground, so we descended again to get a better look at the scenery below.

I marveled at the limitless possibilities technology offered on Guoke. Here, one's imagination seemed to be the only boundary. I wondered aloud if there were rivers on the planet, and Weili smiled.

"There are many rivers and lakes on Guoke," she replied. "Let's go see one now."

We descended once more, arriving at a winding river. Its banks were clearly man-made, covered in some smooth, plastic-like material. The water was pristine, and the whole scene looked untouched by pollution.

We moved on to a larger river, then to a massive lake. Along its shores, we saw various animals basking in the sun, like Earth creatures but distinctly alien. Large, lumpy creatures lay lazily on the rocks, resembling bloated grubs, indifferent to our presence.

Suddenly, a jet of water shot from beneath a nearby rock, scattering the sunbathing animals into the air. We realized there was a massive water creature lurking beneath the surface, its mouth wide enough to swallow several of the animals whole.

Fearful of what might happen next, I suggested we leave.

"We should go," Weili agreed. "The water monster won't be satisfied with those animals—it might find you, with your large size, a nice meal."

Before I could respond, we were already back at Weili's home, the danger behind us.

Chapter 18: Underwater Adventure

After a restful night back at Weili's house, we woke up the next day ready for another adventure. I suggested heading to the beach — I'd always wanted to see a vast ocean, something I had never experienced on Earth, and I was curious about what the seas of Guoke Planet looked like.

Weili, however, had an even bolder suggestion: why not explore the ocean floor itself? It sounded thrilling, but how would we do it? Would we need a submarine? What did a Guoke submarine even look like? Surely, it would be more advanced than anything on Earth. I wasn't sure how she planned to make this happen, but since it was her idea, I figured she had a plan. So, I agreed.

"We're using a submarine, right?" I asked.

"Yes," she replied with a sly smile.

"What does it look like? Is it anything like the ones we have on Earth?"

Weili just smiled and said, "You'll see."

With that, we used the global transport system to instantly arrive at a massive building. It was enormous — so tall and wide that I couldn't see the end of it, and certainly, there was no ocean in sight. Confused, I wondered if we had come to the wrong place. Shouldn't we be at the shore with submarines ready for rent?

Weili must have sensed my confusion. "We'll get to the ocean from here. The submarines are inside."

Curious and intrigued, I followed her inside. The moment we entered, we were greeted by a half-human, half-fish hologram — the digital mascot of the building. It was a beautiful girl with a mermaid tail and a spear, floating mid-air. Next to her, glowing Guoke symbols floated, and I could only assume she was welcoming us. Weili ignored the hologram, and we continued deeper into the building.

As we walked through, I noticed the interior was not only grand but intricately designed. The walls were metallic and gleamed like glass, and everything felt futuristic and elegant. We stopped at a particular room, and Weili placed her hand on her ear, communicating with the global information network. A door slid open, revealing a sleek, circular room. Inside, there was a platform in the center, made of something transparent that resembled glass but seemed sturdier and more refined.

The door closed behind us, and suddenly, I felt a soft tug as black, flexible tubes descended from the ceiling, gently lifting Weili and me and setting us down on the platform. Then, the platform began to spin and descend into the floor, like we were sinking into a hidden tunnel. Just when I thought the submarine would finally appear, a small, soap-like red object emerged from the wall.

"What's that?" I asked.

"It's called information mud," she replied casually.

"Information mud? What does it do?"

"It can transform into anything you need."

"Anything? Can it even turn into something as big as you?"

"It can if we had enough of it, but not with this small amount. And it wouldn't work on Earth, anyway — without the global network to power it, it's just a lump of nothing."

I hesitated for a moment, suspicious of what this "mud" would do to me. But trusting Weili, I ate the strange substance.

Almost immediately, I felt a surge of power course through me, like my body was ready to burst with energy. I looked down to see red, thread-like tendrils growing rapidly from my skin, reaching out toward the edges of the platform. The sensation was so overwhelming that I stumbled and fell.

Before I could grasp what was happening, Weili removed her virtual clothes and climbed on top of me. Her skin, cool and impossibly smooth, was pressed against mine. She was smiling mischievously, and although I was still confused by what was happening, I couldn't resist her. We tangled together, and soon, a thick, milk-white substance began to fill the platform, flowing around us.

The liquid began to transform, rapidly shaping itself into what looked like a massive, living submarine—one that resembled a sleek, predatory shark. It became clear that this "submarine" wasn't mechanical but organic. I realized that the red tendrils growing from me had merged with this living machine. I could see through its eyes, feel the water with its fins, and sense the world with its tail as if they were my own limbs.

We had transformed into the submarine, and now we were ready to dive.

The platform continued to lower until we were submerged in water. We were now in the ocean depths of Guoke Planet. As I looked around, I could see other shark-like submarines emerging from circular openings in the massive structure above us. Their graceful movements contrasted sharply with the bulky submarines I'd imagined.

My thoughts were interrupted by the sudden sound of music in my ears. It was a strange, low-pitched beat that made my chest vibrate. Then, a voice from the global network greeted me: "Welcome to the underwater mode of the global information network. Please select the ocean region you would like to explore."

Before I could respond, Weili suggested, "Let's go to Kurna Trench."

The moment I said the name, we were instantly transported, thanks to the global network's power. It was incredible — no need for maps or navigation; we were simply there.

We began our underwater exploration, rising briefly to the surface to enjoy the view of the calm, vast sea before diving deeper into the ocean's mysterious depths. However, Weili seemed more interested in teasing me than exploring. She started playfully provoking me, her smooth body slipping against mine, turning our journey into something much more personal. After some time, we finally steadied ourselves and resumed our exploration.

We entered a series of artificial tunnels carved into the ocean floor, twisting through an underwater mountain. The tunnels were lined with sculptures — rows of human heads carved into pillars. We passed through them, sliding along the slick, smooth walls, occasionally feeling soft, worm-like creatures brush against us. Some tunnels even sprayed us with strange, silky liquids.

As we swam out of the tunnels, a cluster of glowing red creatures swarmed toward us. At first, I thought they were harmless, but when they struck our living submarine, I felt a sharp pain run through my body.

"Did you feel that?" I asked Weili.

"No," she replied. "The red threads you have are connected to the submarine. They let you feel everything it does, but I'm not affected."

I learned that these red threads allowed me to control the submarine, while Weili saw the world through the global network. The deeper we went, the more surreal the scenery became—oddly shaped fish, mysterious glowing plants, and even parts of ancient, massive ruins hidden on the ocean floor.

Suddenly, something far more dangerous appeared: a sleek, silver fish with razor-sharp teeth. I approached cautiously, but the global network's voice warned me, "Danger: Javelin Fish—mechanical harm, non-toxic."

Ignoring the warning, I got closer, and just as I did, the fish shot one of its teeth at me like a harpoon. I felt a piercing pain in my back as the fish retrieved its tooth. For a moment, I panicked, thinking the living submarine was damaged beyond repair, but the network assured me it was healing itself.

That was just the beginning. We soon encountered a massive creature resembling a woman, half-submerged in the ocean floor. Her form was both beautiful and terrifying, with her body extending into the sea like a sleeping giant.

She locked eyes with me, and I felt an eerie sense of danger.

"She's a high-level sea creature," Weili explained. "She could easily overpower us. Let's get out of here."

But I couldn't help but ask, "What does she want? Would she eat me?"

"No, not like you're thinking," Weili said. "If she catches you, she'll make you her slave, and you'll never escape. She'll keep you as a prisoner, using her strange, powerful body to trap you in endless pleasure until you're nothing but a shell of yourself."

Horrified, I followed Weili's advice, and we quickly fled the creature's territory. We encountered even more bizarre lifeforms, from snake-like beings with human faces to strange hybrid creatures that blurred the line between plants and animals.

The ocean of Guoke Planet was as breathtaking as it was terrifying, and after narrowly escaping several dangerous encounters, I decided I'd had enough.

"Weili, let's go back," I said, exhausted.

She smiled and nodded. "Time to head home."

In a blink, we were back at the starting point. The living submarine dissolved into a pool of white liquid, the red threads disappearing from my body. We stepped out of the room, and just like that, our underwater adventure was over.

But the memories of the strange and wondrous things I had seen would linger with me forever.

Chapter 19: Invasion of the Sea Serpents

After Weili and I returned from our underwater adventure, we shared our experience with Norton and Sudair. When I mentioned the sea serpents, Norton's eyes lit up. He revealed that sea serpents were one of his research subjects and suggested that we take a flying saucer back to the ocean to study them more closely. I was hesitant but didn't really have a choice — Norton's excitement was contagious, and before I knew it, I found myself tagging along. What I didn't realize at the time was that I might have walked right into one of Norton's traps.

The saucer descended silently into the ocean, slipping beneath the waves like a cloud passing through the sky. We began our observations through a 3D virtual display, watching the underwater world unfold before us. As we approached the sea serpents' territory, the display zoomed in, giving us the sensation of peering through an enormous glass wall into the ocean depths.

This part of the ocean wasn't very deep, and sunlight filtered through the water, illuminating the seabed in clear, sharp detail. From a distance, the sea serpents looked like writhing whips, thousands of them swaying gently on the ocean floor. The center of the colony was a dull, withered yellow, while the outer edges were a vibrant pink.

"Those in the center are already dead," Norton explained. "The ones around the edge are young, energetic females."

He continued, explaining that these serpents, much like plants, derive energy from sunlight. However, unlike traditional plants, their method of harnessing energy was far more complex. The sea serpents, a species somewhere between plants and animals, were parasitic in nature. The female serpents were known to invade male bodies, causing high fevers and dissolving their internal organs. But in return, they provided intense, euphoric pleasure. In the end, both the male host and the serpent would die together.

I couldn't understand the point — was their entire existence a slow wait for a mutual death? The idea seemed senseless to me, but I kept my thoughts to myself.

As our saucer drew closer, the serpents became clearer. These creatures were slender, with long, snake-like bodies. Their waists were impossibly thin — narrower than my arm—and they had two small, pointed breasts and visible genitalia. Their skin was soft, vibrant pink, like the tongue of a newborn baby, and their bodies were covered in a crisscrossing pattern of red, black, and white scales, much like the snakes back on Earth.

Their faces, however, were disturbingly human. They had sharp, angular eyes that tilted upward at the corners, giving them a mischievous look. Their mouths and noses were small, but their lips curved with a devilish grin. Thin, flexible tendrils extended from their heads, adding to their eerie allure.

Norton suggested that we leave the saucer and observe the serpents up close. Before I could protest, I saw that Norton, Sudair, and Weili were already outside the saucer, each enveloped in what looked like a transparent bubble, allowing them to breathe normally. I reluctantly followed, and soon found myself wrapped in the same protective bubble of air.

The moment we approached, the serpents went wild. Their bodies began thrashing rhythmically, as if performing a seductive dance, their faces now more enticing and dangerous.

I hung back, filled with fear. Norton had warned that these serpents could burrow into our bodies and dissolve our organs. The thought alone made my blood run cold. I chose a flat spot a bit further from the action, hoping to avoid drawing attention. But my hope was short-lived.

For some unknown reason, my protective bubble suddenly ruptured, breaking apart into tiny air bubbles that floated toward the surface. I was immediately submerged in the cold, salty water, gasping for air that was no longer there. To make matters worse, the nearest serpents noticed me. Their wild movements stirred the water, and I found myself drifting helplessly toward them.

Looking around, I realized Norton, Sudair, and the saucer had vanished. Panic set in as I realized there was no one left to help me. Closing my eyes, I prayed that this was all a nightmare—that when I opened them again, I'd be safe in Weili's bed.

But when I opened my eyes, I wasn't in bed. I was floating above the serpents, their tendrils already reaching for me. They quickly wrapped around my legs, their cold, slimy bodies coiling tighter and tighter. It felt like being trapped in a nest of chicken intestines. Soon, my arms and waist were wrapped too, and the pressure intensified. I couldn't breathe, couldn't fight back. The few parts of my body that weren't entwined felt the serpents licking and rubbing me, their tongues slithering across my skin.

I stopped struggling, realizing it was useless, and tried to convince myself this was still just a dream. But the serpents wouldn't let me retreat into that illusion. They pried my eyes open with their sharp, forked tongues, forcing me to look at them. Their heads were small, but their mouths stretched unnervingly wide, revealing sharp, needle-like teeth. Their tongues, long and purple-black, moved with terrifying agility.

One of the serpents forced itself into my mouth, filling it with a foul, sticky liquid. The taste and smell were revolting, and I gagged, unable to resist. Another serpent tightened around my neck, squeezing so hard that it felt like my throat was being crushed. The one inside me continued its invasion, slithering down into my stomach, where it released a flood of viscous liquid, causing a burning sensation that made me retch.

Then, as I lay there, overwhelmed by the horror, I realized I could breathe again. Somehow, despite everything, I wasn't suffocating anymore. The serpents around my legs spread wide, far too wide — and I knew what was coming next.

It wasn't long before I felt a soft yet cold tendril push its way into my body through my most vulnerable spot. The serpents, of course, didn't make it easy. Several of them tightened their grip around my abdomen, increasing the pressure and friction, as if they were savoring the sensation.

But as the friction built, something strange happened. Instead of pain, I was flooded with waves of intense pleasure. My body trembled and convulsed uncontrollably. The revolting feeling of their slimy liquid shifted to something else — something almost intoxicating. My throat, stomach, and intestines burned with heat, yet I craved more of their touch.

Was this how they dissolved my organs? Fear mixed with euphoria as I began to wonder if I was already dying. My body felt lighter, almost weightless, as though I was floating toward the surface, surrounded by surreal beauty. I saw visions of beautiful girls with snake-like tails, their naked bodies swaying in a hypnotic dance, wrapping around me, touching me everywhere—inside and out.

Was this the end? Had the serpents begun the process of devouring my body?

Just as I thought I would lose myself completely to the sensation, I felt the serpents' hold loosen. One by one, they peeled off me, as if sliced away by some unseen force.

I awoke to find myself lying on a bed, feeling groggy and weak. The serpents were gone, but my body was still swollen and full of memories of their invasion. I could still feel the remnants of their touch deep inside me, reminding me that it hadn't been a dream.

Norton, Sudair, and Weili were standing nearby. Norton glanced at me and then motioned to a pile of thin, white bones lying on a tray beside the bed.

"See these?" Norton said. "These are the serpents' skeletons. Without our help, you wouldn't have been able to expel them from your body."

I looked at the delicate, fish-like bones, shivering at the memory of how they had once been inside me. Norton didn't ask me how it felt to be invaded by the sea serpents, but I could tell by the look in his eyes that he knew exactly what I had been through.

Chapter 20: Touring the Guoke Planet Artificial Field Launch Center

The most important infrastructure on Guoke Planet is the Artificial Field Launch Center, which powers the planet's incredible instant teleportation technology through its global movement network. Finally, I got the chance to visit this place with Weili, Norton, and Sudair.

I asked where the launch center was located, and Sudair pointed to the sky. Even in broad daylight, I could see a silver-gray satellite shining brightly above us. With the help of the global movement network, we instantly transported to the Artificial Field Launch Center.

When we arrived, I was struck by the sheer size of the place. It was enormous, with interconnected, sleek metallic rooms in shades of lead gray and silver. The walls glowed with a soft, uniform light, and there weren't any visible light bulbs or the usual virtual structures I had grown accustomed to on Guoke Planet.

"It's huge, like we've landed on another planet. This shouldn't be called an artificial field launch device—it's more like an entire center," I exclaimed.

Sudair nodded, "You're right. This is the Artificial Field Launch Center. Its most important piece of equipment is the artificial field generator. This center not only powers our teleportation system but also supplies the planet with energy and serves as the core of our global information network. Unlike your Earth, we don't use electrical energy; we use field energy."

He continued, "This center is also the energy hub of Guoke Planet, processing and distributing energy from our stars. You could compare it to a solar energy collector on Earth, but it's much more advanced. There are nine of these centers across Guoke Planet, and smaller neighboring planets have six. I work remotely from here through the public information network, but I only visit in person occasionally."

Weili chimed in, "You know, the core part of the launch center is the only place where teleportation doesn't work."

"Ah, I get it. Like how a barber can cut everyone's hair except their own," I said.

Norton added, "What we're feeling as gravity here is actually artificial, generated by the center."

As we walked, I noticed that most of the workers were about one meter tall, their gazes turning to us — perhaps because I stood out with my height. They whispered among themselves, but the global public information network didn't translate their words for me, so I was left wondering what they were talking about.

Suddenly, our bodies lifted off the ground about 30 centimeters, and we began floating through the air, moving swiftly. We entered a cruising mode and soon reached the heart of the Artificial Field Launch Center. Sudair pointed to an enormous ring-shaped structure.

"This is the core of the artificial field generator—a particle circulation device. The diameter is about 10 kilometers, and the tube itself is nearly a kilometer wide. The rest of the equipment supports it, including the stellar energy collector, which we'll see shortly," Sudair explained.

I asked, "So how does this whole system work?"

"It's similar to how our flying saucers operate. It's all based on creating positive and negative gravitational fields by manipulating electromagnetic fields, which affect the surrounding space and time…"

Before Norton could finish explaining, we were interrupted by the arrival of the center's staff, likely managers, who came to greet him and Sudair. They went into a meeting room, leaving Weili to guide me around the facility.

Still curious, I turned to Weili. "How can flying saucers and the launch center work on the same principle?"

"Both the saucers and the artificial field generators consume the surrounding space, manipulating the mass and electric charge distribution of objects in that space to make them move," Weili said softly, though her words were still a bit beyond me.

"And how do they consume the space around them?"

"By generating changing electromagnetic fields that create positive and negative gravitational fields. The anti-gravitational field travels at the speed of light, affecting the space around objects, which makes the mass and electric charge disappear. The object is then excited, moving at light speed and exhibiting all sorts of strange properties… That's as much as I know," Weili admitted.

As she spoke, she playfully wrapped her arms around my neck, tilting her head to meet my eyes. "Any more questions?" she asked in a teasing voice.

"What exactly is a field?"

"A field is a space in spiral motion, like a cylinder… Do you have any more questions?" Weili's voice was soft, yet playful.

Feeling a flutter in my chest, I didn't ask any more questions. Weili, as usual, was affectionate, clinging to me like a cat. She loved to float in the air, using the global movement network to keep herself at my height. Sometimes, she hovered so that her face was at the level of my waist, curling around me like a slippery eel, or she'd ride on my shoulders, her smooth body pressing against me.

It was difficult to maintain my composure, especially since our clothing was merely virtual projections, meaning we were actually naked. Weili didn't seem to care, nor did Norton or Sudair. They acted as if everything was perfectly normal, leaving me feeling embarrassed. When I asked Weili to keep her distance, she would ignore me, yet when I tried to get closer, she'd teasingly move away. It was impossible to understand the logic behind her actions.

We floated hand-in-hand to the top of the particle circulation device, where the stellar energy collector was located. Unlike the imposing ring of the particle device, the energy collector was a flat surface covered with concentric circles. In the center of each circle was a black dot, possibly a hole or some other material. From a distance, it was hard to tell.

I wanted to get a closer look, but Weili stopped me. "It's dangerous to get too close. Even if you wanted to, you couldn't reach it."

"This device collects stellar energy by focusing the sunlight from the star, right?" I asked.

"Exactly. While your solar panels on Earth can only capture the energy that falls on them, this collector compresses the space around it, so that each square meter can capture energy equivalent to thousands or even millions of square meters."

"That's impressive! But what if a spacecraft flies over it? Wouldn't it get destroyed by the collector?"

"There's a risk, but we've already accounted for that. The collector works on a grid system, dividing the space into sections, so it doesn't affect spacecraft passing by."

"Grid system?"

Weili smiled and drew crisscrossing lines in the air. "See? You're smart—you get it."

I nodded, pretending to understand. "So, this collector can also control the amount of solar energy hitting different parts of the planet, right?"

"Yes, that's right. By adjusting the amount of stellar energy each area receives, we can regulate the planet's atmosphere, keeping the climate in balance. Since we don't wear real clothes with thermal insulation, controlling the weather is essential. It's like putting the whole planet inside a giant air conditioner. That way, we avoid extreme weather events like hurricanes, storms, and floods, which you still must deal with on Earth."

I sighed. "It would be amazing if we had something like this on Earth. We'd save so many lives."

Weili laughed. "Then why don't you go back and build one? You'd be the richest man on Earth!"

After reuniting with Norton and Sudair, we prepared to leave. As we walked, I noticed something odd — some rooms in the facility seemed to be directly connected to outer space. The air should have been rushing out, but it wasn't.

Curious, I asked Sudair, "Why doesn't the air escape into space?"

He pointed to the door. "Go ahead, touch it."

I cautiously approached the door and reached out. My hand met an invisible barrier — a virtual wall, it turned out. The wall wasn't visible, which had confused me earlier.

We used the global movement network to teleport back to Weili's home. My mind was still spinning with all the unanswered questions about the artificial field generator, but I could tell from their casual demeanor that Norton, Weili, and Sudair weren't interested in discussing it further. With a sigh, I let the matter drop and joined their conversation about something else entirely.

Chapter 21: The Light Virtual Beings

One day, while walking with Norton, Sudair, and Weili, I noticed something unusual: a group of Guoke people whose bodies seemed to have no weight, moving in an almost floating manner. At first glance, they looked like ordinary Guoke citizens, but their lightness and the way they moved caught my attention. Suddenly, these people drifted through the walls of a building as if the walls offered no resistance at all.

I immediately thought that perhaps the global movement network was helping them, but that network usually works so fast that you don't notice the process. My instinct told me there was something different about these people.

"Those people are so strange. How did they just pass through that wall? Can you do that too?" I asked, feeling both intrigued and puzzled.

Weili, as usual, seemed unfazed. "Those people are Light Virtual Beings. You've seen them before at Norton's place."

"Oh, so buildings can be virtual, and people can be too?" I spoke. "But I've noticed virtual buildings always have a slight shimmer to them. These people didn't seem to have that effect."

Weili explained, "Buildings don't require much precision, so the imaging can be a bit rough. But for virtual people, the imaging is much finer. When it reaches a certain level of detail, you can't see any shimmer."

Despite her explanation, I was still confused. Norton noticed my baffled expression and decided to give a more technical explanation.

"Virtual beings on Guoke Planet originated from our development of artificial field scanning technology," he began. "This allowed us to scan the human brain and record a person's thoughts and consciousness. Initially, we stored these in computers, hoping that one day we'd be able to transfer the consciousness into an artificial body, effectively allowing us to live forever by switching into new, younger bodies.

But from the beginning, these recorded consciousnesses weren't just sitting idle in computers. They were running as active programs. This was the birth of the first Virtual Beings."

Norton continued, "At first, these beings only existed in our network. To interact with them, we needed screens and displays to see their avatars, and they lacked a cohesive, human form. But as technology advanced, particularly with the development of 3D imaging and artificial field scanning, Virtual Beings could step out of the network and into the real world as projections.

The Light Virtual Beings you saw today are created by locking local light and color through field scanning technology and combining it with 3D imaging."

"So, the light around them is manipulated to create the image of a person?" I asked.

"Yes, but it's more complex than that," Norton explained. "The global movement network and the global information network both play a role in tracking and supporting these beings. The data flow needed to sustain a Virtual Being is immense, requiring computational power billions of times greater than what your Earth computers are capable of."

I was beginning to grasp it. "So, these Virtual Beings are essentially collections of data that look like people, but they have no real bodies?"

"Exactly," Norton said. "Although their bodies are made of light, they possess self-awareness, and their consciousness functions just like ours, stored as data in a computer and running continuously. They can communicate with each other, form relationships, even fall in love. Some Virtual Beings use special tools like 'information mud' to engage in physical activities like sex with either other Virtual Beings or real, physical people."

Weili added, "They have all the thoughts and emotions we do, but their experiences in the physical world are very different. They don't need to eat or drink, and they can't feel pain because they don't have physical bodies. However, they do experience emotions, and they can suffer from mental anguish just like us."

Norton continued, "Virtual Beings can't perceive the world the way we do. They don't experience hunger or thirst, and they never get sick. But they do feel happiness and even sexual pleasure. They can move from place to place more freely than we can, passing through walls or floating in the air, because physical objects don't obstruct them. They have no concept of barriers."

I was amazed. "So, they're like beings living in a different dimension, able to move through space as they wish?"

Sudair chimed in, "Most people on Guoke Planet are Virtual Beings."

That statement startled me. "So Virtual Beings are just people who gave up on reality, hiding in a digital world?"

Weili shook her head. "No, everyone here has both a physical body and a virtual identity. You can choose to appear as a Virtual Being or as a real person—it's all up to you."

"Wait, so everyone can live in both forms?" I asked, astonished.

"Exactly," Weili said. "In some cases, a person can have multiple bodies or virtual identities at once. You're not limited to a human body either—you could be a spaceship, a fish, or even a castle. These forms are fully intelligent and capable of interacting with people. They're not lifeless objects."

Norton added, "Most people prefer to use their physical bodies for day-to-day life, but some choose to stay as Virtual Beings for long periods of time."

Back at Weili's place, I couldn't stop asking about the Virtual Beings. I was fascinated, and Weili, in a rare mood of patience, explained everything in detail.

I asked, "Does every Virtual Being have a backup body to return to when they want to be physical again?"

"Yes, that's right," Weili said, showing me images of transparent pods filled with liquid, each containing a sleeping person. Some of the bodies inside were of beautiful women, which made my heart race. Weili noticed my reaction and smirked.

"Do all Virtual Beings have a body stored like this?" I asked.

"Not always," she said. "Very few people actually switch back to their physical bodies. It's rare."

"What if I want to be both—real and virtual at the same time?"

Weili shook her head. "That would split your consciousness, causing confusion and mental anguish. No one wants that."

Finally, tired of my endless questions, Weili handed me a simulation program. "Why don't you experience it yourself?" she suggested.

As I lay down, I suddenly found myself in a surreal world. The surroundings looked like painted landscapes, with Guoke symbols floating in the sky. As I walked, a voice asked, "Where would you like to go? Do you need a companion? Please make your selection."

On the side of the road stood five beautiful women, all eagerly waving at me. Each was stunning, but strangely, I found myself drawn to one who reminded me of Weili. I chose her, but as soon as I did, the others disappeared, leaving me alone with my choice.

With a new group of floating pets following me, I embarked on an adventure. Every now and then, a voice would prompt me to make decisions, and while I made mistakes and had to retrace my steps, I was slowly learning how to navigate this strange virtual world.

The most incredible part was the freedom. I could leap across mountains, glide through walls, and even float in the air. At one point, I turned to the woman beside me and embraced her. A surge of pleasure washed over me. Then, as if waking from a dream, I opened my eyes to find Weili standing in front of me, watching.

Over time, I played this virtual game in various settings, experiencing the life of a Virtual Being again and again.

The virtual world was full of wonders. Without the weight of gravity, my body felt as light as a feather, and I could soar through the sky or phase through solid walls. Everything around me was in constant motion, the colors shifting and blending. Time, space, and the rules of reality seemed to dissolve. In this realm, you could fly, split into countless particles, or merge with someone else, dissolving into each other's form.

Virtual Beings lived without the need for food, drink, or sleep. They could move instantly from one place to another, unbound by physical limitations. The dangers of the real world—fire, water, or even deadly falls—posed no threat to them.

And though they had no physical form, Virtual Beings could still feel love, form relationships, and even engage in sexual experiences. These beings were not just shadows of humanity — they were living, breathing souls, free from the constraints of the physical world.

Yet, even in this incredible existence, they were not free from pain. Emotional pain still haunted them. And in a way, I realized, their world was just as complex and layered as ours.

The light Virtual Beings of Guoke Planet were a reflection of the limitless possibilities of the mind and the power of technology to transcend physical boundaries. And while their world was alluring, I knew there would always be something grounding me in the physical world — something real.

Chapter 22: Guoke Planet's Space-Time Refrigerator

One day, while eating at Weili's place, I had some leftover food. I said, "Back on Earth, we would store this in the refrigerator. We didn't have one in my village because we were poor, but I saw in movies that city people all had refrigerators. Hey, Weili, I haven't noticed any refrigerators on Guoke Planet. Oh, I get it, your technology is so advanced — you don't need to store food because of your instant transportation systems, right?"

Weili smiled. "We actually do have refrigerators, but they're very large and rarely used for food. Our refrigerators serve different purposes than those on Earth."

I thought I understood. "Ah, so you have massive refrigerators, more like public warehouses where everyone stores their stuff. Then when someone needs something, they use the global movement network to retrieve it instantly, just like having it at home. That way, you save energy and space, right?"

Weili shook her head slightly. "Not exactly. On Guoke Planet, the nutrients our bodies need are directly transferred into us through the global movement network, controlled by a computer program. We don't usually need food, so refrigerators for food are unnecessary. Our refrigerators are mainly used in industrial production and scientific research."

As she spoke, Weili gestured in the air, and the global information network created a three-dimensional virtual image beside her. She opened the network, revealing images of massive refrigerators across Guoke Planet, each looking like a building, labeled with Guokean symbols.

Weili continued, "Our refrigerators don't work by freezing things at low temperatures like yours on Earth. Instead, we use a method that freezes time itself. We call them Space-Time Refrigerators. We use artificial fields to freeze the flow of time inside the refrigerator. So, while a minute might pass inside, years—or even thousands of years—could pass outside.

For example, if you put an ice cream cone inside one of our space-time refrigerators, the temperature inside wouldn't be any different from outside. But while a year passes for us, only a second might pass inside. So, when you take out the ice cream a year later, it's still as fresh as when you put it in."

"Wow! That's incredible! I never would have imagined that" I exclaimed. "So, if I went inside one of these refrigerators, stayed for a while, and came out, thousands of years might have passed outside?"

Weili laughed. "Yes, on Earth, if you went into a regular fridge, you might freeze to death. But in our space-time fridge, you wouldn't freeze. However, when you come out, everyone you know—your family, neighbors—would be long gone, thousands of years passed. You'd become an ancient artifact, with people lining up to stare at you like you're a museum exhibit or a zoo attraction."

I laughed at the absurdity of it. "What if I wanted the opposite? Could I spend a year in the fridge, but only a few hours pass outside?"

"That's possible too," Weili said. "Our space-time refrigerators have adjustable settings. If you set it on low, a minute inside might equal a year outside. On high, a minute inside could mean thousands of years outside. And if you press the space-time inversion switch, you reverse the flow — time moves faster inside and slower outside."

"Can it reverse time? Like, could I go back to the past?" I asked, intrigued.

"No, time can't flow backward," Weili said firmly. "Time is relative. You can only compare the speed of time between two places. You can't compare yourself to yourself, but you can compare your height to mine. That's how time works — it only moves forward."

Her explanation made some sense, but I still had questions. "So, what is time exactly?"

Weili replied, "Time is just our perception of space expanding outward at the speed of light. Without people, there's no time. But if you want to know more, you should ask Sudair or Norton."

Later, Weili suggested we visit a biological research facility where they used these giant space-time refrigerators. I agreed, and she contacted the head of the research institute, letting him know that an Earthling wanted to visit.

"Norton is a famous biologist here on Guoke Planet. Let's invite him to join us," Weili said.

"Sure," I agreed.

In the blink of an eye, thanks to the global movement network, we arrived in front of a massive building. Norton was already there, waiting with a virtual greeter — a half-human, half-insect figure with green and yellow stripes on its lower half.

As we entered, the staff treated Norton with great respect. Weili whispered that they were all under

Norton's leadership. Soon, we were greeted by a man named Wentai, who had long black hair that looked like soft tubes draped over his shoulders. Weili hinted that his hair had a special purpose in enhancing pleasure during intimate moments with women but didn't elaborate further, leaving me to imagine it.

Wentai led us through the facility, excitedly explaining everything in rapid speech. The global information network's translation service struggled to keep up, but I wasn't too interested in the technical details of the bizarre equipment. I was more fascinated by the rows of transparent containers filled with slightly yellowish liquid, where all sorts of naked human bodies floated.

Some were enormous, standing four or five meters tall, while others were tiny, barely a few centimeters in height. I even saw a female body that looked distinctly Earth-like—tall, voluptuous, and strangely alluring. Tubes connected to her back, and her expression was peaceful, as though in a deep sleep.

Weili must have noticed my curious gaze because she suddenly tapped me and muttered something that the translation service didn't catch. I figured it was probably a Guokean curse word.

Wentai explained, "These bodies are backups for Guokeans who may need them for special missions. Sometimes, when we go to Earth, we need a body that blends in with humans. So, we transfer a Guokean's consciousness into one of these Earth-like bodies and store their original body here. Once the mission is over, we reverse the process."

"Why do they all have tubes connected to them?" I asked.

"The tubes are part of a life-support system," Wentai explained. "They provide nutrition, remove waste, and maintain vital functions. Most of this is done through the global movement network, but the tubes help regulate other processes. The containers are essentially space-time refrigerators. Outside, years might pass, but inside, barely a few seconds go by."

"Why not make it so that no time passes at all inside?" I asked.

Norton stepped in to explain. "The larger the time difference, the more energy it takes to maintain the field. The equipment would need to be enormous, and the system becomes unstable. That's why we don't freeze time completely."

As we moved deeper into the facility, we saw even larger, non-transparent space-time refrigerators. These had virtual screens attached, showing fast-forwarded scenes from inside. It looked like the daily life of people, but everything was moving at an impossible speed.

Wentai explained, "This refrigerator runs faster inside than outside. The people you see are living out years in just a few of our hours. We use this to study the natural evolution of life."

Norton added, "We observe how viruses, bacteria, and other organisms evolve over long periods. It's essential for our biological research."

"Is this where you store most of the backup bodies?" I asked.

Wentai shook his head. "No, this facility is more for experimentation. Our main storage is in the body replication factories, where there are tens of thousands of bodies in reserve. This is just a small lab."

Weili, clearly eager to leave, wrapped her arm around mine and said, "We'll take you to the replication factories someday—that'll really blow your mind. But for now, let's go. There's nothing that interesting here. It's just a few bodies in tanks."

We left the research facility, but the concept of the space-time refrigerators stayed with me, sparking endless questions. As we returned to Weili's place, I realized just how advanced and different Guokean technology was from anything I could've imagined back on Earth.

Chapter 23: A Visit to the Guoke Planet Human Replication Factory

One day, Weili said, "Qian Ge, remember I promised to take you to see the human replication factory here on Guoke Planet? Norton just sent me a message through the global information network saying he has some business at the factory. He's asking if you'd like to come along. Would you like to visit the factory with us?"

"Yes, I'd love to!" I responded eagerly.

Weili immediately linked to the global information network through her mind, sending a message to Norton. Moments later, both Norton and Sudair appeared on Weili's virtual sofa via the global movement network.

"We're going to the human replication factory soon. Can Qian Ge join us?" Norton asked me.

"Of course! Are we going right now?" I replied.

"We need to wait a bit," Norton explained. "The head of the factory, Gapon, hasn't arrived yet. He'll let us know when he's there, and then we'll go."

Curious, I asked, "So what exactly do they make in the human replication factory? Do they create mannequins? What materials do they use? Plastic?"

Sudair burst into laughter. "Oh, come on! What kind of thoughts are those?" He continued, "The Guoke Planet Human Replication Factory is the largest and most important facility we have. It specializes in replicating living human bodies."

Weili chimed in with pride, "On Earth, people dream of immortality and look for some magical elixir, but no such thing exists in the universe. Here on Guoke Planet, when our bodies grow old or become weak, we simply replace them with younger ones, preserving our consciousness. This way, we stay young forever and achieve immortality!"

Skeptical, I turned to Norton, "But if you get a new body, is it really still you?"

"Absolutely," Norton said firmly. "The essence of a person is their consciousness and thoughts. The body is secondary. We view humans as two parts— one is the consciousness, the other is the body. Consciousness is the electrical activity in the brain, essentially information. The body is just like hardware, like the way computers have hardware like monitors, keyboards, and storage devices. Consciousness is like software or data on a computer."

He continued, "When a person's body grows old or sick, we scan their brain with artificial field technology and copy their consciousness into digital form, storing it in a computer. Then we grow a new, blank human body and transfer the consciousness back into this new brain. The old body is safely disposed of, and the person wakes up in a fresh, young body, with all memories intact. When this new body grows old, we do it again. By repeating the process, Guokeans live forever."

"That makes sense," I said. "It's like fixing a bicycle tire. You can patch it up, but if it's too damaged, you replace it entirely. You're doing the same with bodies—when they get too old or damaged, you switch to a new one but keep the consciousness."

Weili nodded. "Exactly."

At that moment, Norton received a message. "Gapon has arrived at the factory," he announced. "Let's go."

In an instant, Weili, Sudair, Norton, and I were transported to the Guoke Planet Human Replication Factory.

The factory's virtual greeter appeared as a common male Guokean, but with his body split in half, each side moving in perfect synchronization. The building itself was enormous, stretching as far as the eye could see, with large virtual lettering above the entrance.

"Wow, this place is huge!" I exclaimed.

"This is just one of the entrances," Sudair said dismissively.

Inside, the factory complex was a marvel — beautiful, with strange plants, vibrant flowers, and virtual three-dimensional imagery everywhere. Each building had virtual Guokean text floating above it. We climbed into a floating car that hovered about two meters above the ground, silently gliding through the air.

After a while, Norton left to meet with Gapon, leaving us to continue the tour. We eventually arrived at a massive building with a few people moving around inside. We got out of the floating car and found Norton talking with Gapon.

Gapon was about a meter tall, with a strong, stocky build. He greeted me warmly, shaking my hand and commenting on my size.

"You're big, Qian Ge! You must be very strong," he said. Then, with a playful grin, he asked, "With such a large body, how do you and Weili manage in bed? When you're together, who has more stamina?"

To illustrate his point, Gapon made a crude gesture with his hands, mimicking a sexual act. I could see Weili's face flush with anger as she quickly separated her hands in a dismissive motion.

"There's nothing like that happening!" she snapped, clearly irritated by his behavior.

Gapon, still amused, backed off a little but continued teasing. "Really? Well, why did you bring him all the way from Earth? Isn't it to study his sexual relations with us, to gather useful data? Isn't that right, Norton?"

Norton didn't respond. Weili, with her head held high, began walking around, swaying like a proud princess. I followed, along with Sudair.

Gapon finally caught up with us and began explaining the factory's equipment and features. His hand gestures and animated explanations made it clear he was passionate about the place, but I found myself thinking back to the bodies floating in yellow liquid at the biological research institute. I wondered if I'd see such sights here again.

Finally, we reached the underground part of the factory, where rows of transparent containers held naked bodies in a pale-yellow liquid, all with tubes connecting to their bodies. Unlike the research institute, these bodies were uniform in size and height, all around one meter tall.

"These are our backup bodies," Gapon explained. "Whenever someone needs to change bodies, we use one of these."

"Why the tubes?" I asked.

"They provide nutrients and remove waste. Though most of this is handled by the global movement network, we still need a system for basic biological functions," Gapon replied.

I was curious. "Why not use your instant transfer technology to handle all of it?"

Gapon explained, "The tubes are part of a life-support system that maintains bodily functions. These bodies are like blank canvases, without any consciousness, so we need to ensure they stay in perfect condition."

I looked around, fascinated. "Why are all the bodies the same size? Why not have larger or smaller ones for variety?"

Gapon smiled. "Uniformity makes manufacturing easier, like on Earth where products are made to standard sizes. Also, after extensive research, we've found that this size is optimal for our planet's gravity and environment. It's perfect for physical activities, including sex and disease resistance."

He added, "Another reason is to prevent size disparities from causing harm. Large bodies could potentially hurt smaller ones. On Guoke Planet, we don't have laws or moral codes to govern behavior. Sometimes, sex can be violent, so we control the source by making sure body sizes are compatible."

Hearing this, Weili quickly jumped to my side and clung to my arm in an affectionate display. Trying to steer the conversation away from sex, I asked, "How many of these backup bodies do you have?"

"About a few million," Weili answered casually.

"And how many replication factories are there?"

"Just one," Gapon replied. "Human replication is the most important industry on Guoke Planet, so it's centralized."

Curious again, I asked, "If someone switches to a new body, what happens to the old one? Are there two of them now?"

"There would be two, yes, unless we dispose of the old one," Gapon said.

"And how do you do that?" I inquired.

"We kill it and then incinerate it!" Sudair laughed, shaking with mirth.

Weili scolded him. "Sudair, stop using scary language!"

I then asked, "Can you replicate a body for me, as an Earthling?"

"We don't have the program for that," Gapon replied. "It would take a long time to develop, and our laws are strict. We can't replicate extraterrestrial bodies casually."

We continued the tour, and I couldn't help but ask, "What if someone dies unexpectedly? Can you still replicate their body?"

Norton explained, "On Guoke Planet, we back up our consciousness regularly. So even if someone dies, we can restore them with a new body and all their memories up until the last backup."

"Can you modify someone's consciousness during replication?"

"No," Norton replied. "We respect the original consciousness. However, in research facilities, under controlled conditions, we may alter certain aspects for scientific purposes."

By the end of the tour, I was filled with awe and a deeper understanding of Guokean immortality. Their technology had turned dreams of eternal youth into reality, far beyond anything Earth had achieved.

As we prepared to leave, I remarked, "On Earth, the quest for immortality has been a dream for thousands of years. I wonder how long it will take us to achieve something like this."

Gapon responded, "It's not a matter of time, but understanding. Once you Earthlings understand the nature of consciousness and develop artificial field technology, immortality is within reach."

Norton added, "But you must be willing to let go of old ways of thinking. As long as you're focused on the body and not the mind, you'll never succeed."

And with that, I realized how far humanity still had to go.

Chapter 24: The New Species of Guoke Planet

Not long after our visit to the Guoke Planet's human replication factory, Norton, Sudair, and Weili took me to visit a research center dedicated to the development of new species of humanoids. On Guoke Planet, due to their advanced technology and high level of virtualization, areas like energy, transportation, space exploration, and information processing have been perfected to such an extent that there is little room left for further development.

The Guoke people have a peculiar fascination with altering and creating new bodies for themselves. The most significant focus of their research is the human body, and their largest industry revolves around manufacturing their own bodies. With the ability to copy a person's consciousness from their brain and install it into another body, it's effortless for them to switch bodies and experience life through new forms.

This research center was housed inside a vast building, so high that the ceiling was obscured by some unseen cover. A virtual digital avatar of the center greeted us — a small boy, racing toward us with a glowing rod in his hand, much like Sun Wukong from Chinese legend. He stood in front of us, motionless, as a line of floating Guoke script appeared beside him. Ke Wen, our guide from the global information network, translated it as "Speed Kid," implying that the new humanoid species being developed at this center were incredibly powerful and fast.

However, Norton and the others paid no attention to this digital avatar, marching past it without a second glance.

Inside, I encountered an array of bizarre and unimaginable humanoid species. One of the most striking was a shining black metallic woman. Her skin was cool to the touch and highly elastic, giving her an unusual heaviness. The experience of intimacy with her left me with a lasting memory — her body's friction was like fine grains of sand, a strange yet exhilarating sensation, though it drained my stamina. Some metallic species had bodies that felt like needles pricking my skin, while others carried a faint electrical charge.

Among the various metal-skinned species, I encountered two women standing together, both with the same shiny black metal bodies. They were about a meter tall, completely naked, with slender yet voluptuous frames. The widest parts of their bodies were no thicker than my leg, and their skin was sleek and polished, like steel beams. Their faces were sharp, with small mouths and huge eyes that gleamed eerily like wells reflecting faint light in the darkness.

Norton nudged me forward, urging me to embrace them. Hesitantly, I approached, only for one of the women to release a black, viscous liquid from a slit in her lower body. With a "whoosh," her entire body burst into pale blue flames, which quickly spread to cover her from head to toe. Her companion remained unburned, but I hesitated to make any physical contact, fearing the consequences.

But I had no choice. I embraced the woman who wasn't on fire. To my horror, she leapt onto me, wrapping her legs around my neck. Despite her metallic appearance, her body felt more like the sticky texture of a snail or a leech. Her body opened, releasing an overwhelming odor that mixed the stench of decay with an oddly sweet fragrance. Tendrils emerged from her lower body and began to probe into my mouth and around my body, invading me from every direction.

I felt them winding through my stomach, intestines, and even my colon. Finally, the tendrils exited from my lower body, spraying a black, oily substance like old engine oil over me. Then, with another "whoosh," the woman engulfed me in flames, leaving me to burn alongside her companion.

Though the fire felt more like a warm breeze than actual heat, the experience of having my body invaded by tendrils left me utterly drained. I could feel the blue flames wrapping around us, flickering with silvery threads that swirled into the air. It was an odd sensation, like thousands of small, warm hands gently caressing my body, lulling me into a strange euphoria. Yet, I also felt an encroaching dread, as though everything around me was about to melt away.

When I finally regained consciousness, I found myself back at the center, surrounded by Norton, Sudair, and Weili. More strange species passed by, including some women with eerie, flat faces and eyes that resembled the capital letter "H." Their irises moved in horizontal and vertical lines, adding to their unsettling aura.

Another woman, this one with a slim, frog-like build and bright green skin, practiced jumping in front of us. Her agility was incredible, allowing her to leap many times her own height. Norton struck up a conversation with her, and to my alarm, she approached me with a fierce expression, ready to challenge me.

She was naked, her skin smooth and glistening like polished jade. Her front was a light green, while her back was deep, jade green. Without warning, she leaped onto me, wrapping her legs around my waist and locking me in a tight grip. The strength she exerted was overwhelming, and I felt her tendrils invading my body — both through my mouth and other orifices.

This research center was home to countless creatures of this nature — humanoids capable of splitting their bodies into smaller parts, manipulating the most minute details of their form for invasive, and often terrifying, experiences.

As I explored the center with the others, it became clear that the Guoke people's fascination with creating new bodies wasn't limited to aesthetics. It was an exercise in exploring the boundaries of consciousness, sensation, and physical experience. Their ability to switch bodies, combine human and animal traits, and modify even the most intimate aspects of their being was both fascinating and deeply unsettling.

While Norton explained the logic behind these experiments — balancing human consciousness with physical form — one thing was certain: on Guoke Planet, the line between human and inhuman was perpetually blurred.

Chapter 25: The Tiered Living System of Guoke Planet

One day, Norton, Sudair, and Weili took me to a peculiar region on their home planet. Although still technically on Guoke's main planet, the atmosphere in this area felt distinctly different. The light was dim, and the sky perpetually resembled a stormy overcast, casting everything in a dull, ashen hue. The ground was dotted with thin, glowing strands floating upward, and columns of light in various colors hung suspended in the air, never quite touching the ground.

I couldn't help but wonder, *What kind of technology creates such a strange, surreal atmosphere? It must take a lot of resources to maintain this eerie setting.*

As I gazed upward, a string of giant Guoke characters floated across the sky. Strangely enough, the letters morphed into Chinese characters right before my eyes, displaying a cryptic message:

"Here, death is an illusion, but pain is real."

My mind raced. *What does this mean? Have they customized this place just because they knew a human would be visiting?* I felt uneasy, realizing that these words had been translated specifically for me. Norton and the others, still looking at the Guoke script, remained unaffected, as if it were just another day.

Suddenly, a virtual figure descended to greet us — Guoke's way of providing a digital guide. This one, though, was unsettling: a man with a pained expression, his abdomen filled with gaping holes radiating an ominous glow. His legs were coated with thick, black, tar-like liquid, oozing down toward his feet. Above his head, in more Guoke script, was his name. As I glanced at it, the letters again transformed into Chinese:

"The Melted Man."

Confused and creeped out, I turned to the information guide, Kewen, who explained with unnerving calmness:

"This is an illusion — a mental projection created by the Global Movement Network and the Global Information Network. Anyone who steps into this zone experiences these visions. It's a warning — this place is where females with criminal tendencies tend to gather."

I swallowed hard, suddenly more aware of my surroundings.

"The message you saw in Chinese," Kewen continued, "was generated specifically for you by the networks. Norton and the others are still seeing it in the Guoke language. But there are no physical words in the sky. The dark atmosphere and cryptic messages are crafted as a psychological deterrent. The phrase *'Death is an illusion, but pain is real'* is meant to be a declaration from the women here: 'We can't kill you, but we can make you feel real, excruciating pain.'"

My heart raced. It was becoming clearer what kind of place we had entered.

"The guide you saw — 'The Melted Man' — is a symbolic figure," Kewen explained. "The holes in his body are mockingly symbolic of a man who's been physically damaged during encounters with these women, and the black liquid represents how their toxins 'melt' a man's will and body."

The chilling explanations only heightened my anxiety. According to Kewen, the women who lived here were dangerous—not just in the traditional sense, but in ways that transcended my Earthly understanding. These women could produce potent toxins and had a disturbing love of testing their power on men.

"The Global Networks cannot physically stop certain kinds of behavior," Kewen elaborated. "When a woman uses deceit to engage in harmful sexual activities, the networks cannot immediately separate her from her victim, especially if their bodies are already intertwined."

I had heard enough about the violent nature of the Guoke women, but now I realized that this place was home to those with even darker tendencies. Women here were often categorized as "toxic," and many had been banished to this region because of their uncontainable behavior.

As we walked deeper into this shadowy zone, Norton and the others noticed a target. With a slight grin, they urged me forward, using me as bait. They, of course, hid in the background, watching from a safe distance.

As I approached, I saw a woman standing alone. She was tiny, no taller than a child, with an unnaturally perfect body and delicate features. Her tight top and metallic mini skirt glimmered under the strange, faint light. Her skin was a mix of pale pink and a subtle, dusky blue.

Her hair, smooth and black like polished rubber, fell down in long strands. She looked gentle, innocent even — like a fragile doll. But there was something off about her eyes — something cold, calculating. Her gaze locked on me for a moment, a flash of predatory interest flickering across her face. Then, unexpectedly, she turned and darted off into the distance.

Was I imagining things? Maybe I had misread her. But later, Norton explained that I hadn't been wrong. She had run off to prepare — likely gathering her strength, focusing her toxic energy into her next move. These women were known for their sudden bursts of violence, attacking without warning.

When she returned, she no longer hesitated. Her innocent act vanished as she leaped through the air like a predator. In an instant, her clothes dissolved into nothing, and her naked body glistened in the dim light. Her lower body shot forward, and I barely had time to react before a tendril — her primary weapon — lashed out, striking my abdomen.

I gasped as a hot liquid burned through my skin, numbing my senses and making my vision blur. My thoughts became muddled, and I realized with horror that I had lost control of my body. *She poisoned me.*

Before I could call out for help or try to escape, she was already on me — her legs clamped around my neck, her tendrils wrapping tightly around my face, cutting off my breath. Dozens of smaller tentacles slithered from her body, invading every part of me. Some slipped into my mouth, forcing their way down my throat; others probed deeper, causing an unbearable sensation in my stomach.

She took her time now, moving with slow, deliberate cruelty. She had no interest in simply mating. Her aim was to torment—to push my body and mind to the limit.

As she injected more toxins into my system, my vision swam, and I began to hallucinate. I saw miniature versions of her, dancing through my insides, taunting me as they moved.

In the end, it wasn't the physical pain that broke me—it was the overwhelming, inescapable sense of helplessness. As her tentacles retracted, I was left a shaking, exhausted mess, covered in strange, sticky fluid. My mind spun in confusion, and my body ached in ways I couldn't explain.

When she finally released me and leapt back to the ground, she did so with grace, as if nothing had happened. She walked away casually, leaving me collapsed in a puddle of filth.

Norton and the others eventually came over to help me stand, but I could barely walk. My limbs felt like jelly, and the world around me blurred into a surreal, gray landscape.

As they guided me out of the region, I couldn't help but feel a sense of dread. I knew this wouldn't be the last time I encountered women like her. On Guoke Planet, danger lurked in every corner, and it wasn't just physical — it was psychological, too.

Chapter 26: The Currency of Guoke Planet

One day, I accompanied Weili, Norton, and Sudair to a place they described as an entertainment center. When we entered, I noticed Weili glance at a wall. Immediately, a set of glowing Guoke characters appeared, which quickly vanished as she moved away.

Curious, I asked, "What were you just looking at?"

"I was checking my wealth balance through the Global Information Network," Weili replied.

"Wealth balance? What does that mean?"

"It's essentially the same as checking your bank account on Earth. It shows how much money I have," she explained.

I was taken aback. "But you're so advanced! Why would Guoke Planet even need money? With all your technology, don't you already have everything you need? What's the point of currency?"

Norton chimed in, "Even though we're more technologically advanced than Earth, we still have needs that can't be immediately fulfilled. While material goods are easy to obtain and often free, other services, like asking someone to perform a specific task or access specialized information, still require transactions. Where there's demand, there's trade, and where there's trade, currency follows."

Sudair added, "Money also helps keep our society organized and specialized. Even planets more advanced than ours still rely on some form of currency."

Weili nodded. "However, unlike Earth, our currency is purely digital. You'll never see physical money or coins here. Everything is tracked and handled by the Global Information Network. Whether we earn or spend money, the system records it automatically. When we make a transaction, a virtual figure appears, almost like a personal accountant, keeping track for us. We don't carry cash; our wealth is just a number on the network, easily accessible through either direct brain interface or external devices."

This system seemed mind-boggling to me. "So, say on Earth I dig a hole for my boss, and he hands me cash. How does it work here? If I dig a hole for someone on Guoke, how would I get paid if there's no actual money?"

Weili laughed. "It's simple. The Global Information Network would send a virtual figure to inform you of your earnings. If you were a native Guokean, your brain would immediately register the increase in your wealth. But since you're from Earth and don't fully integrate with our system, it's a bit trickier for you to access your earnings."

"But how do Guoke people earn money?" I asked, still confused.

"In Guoke society, everyone receives a basic, regular income to cover essential needs," Norton explained. "You'll never struggle to survive. But if you want to enjoy luxuries, experience unique things, or simply live a more exciting life, you need to earn extra wealth, and that's much harder. Earning is tightly connected to contributing to the Global Movement Network or the Global

Information Network. Most of our wealth comes from interactions with these networks."

He continued, "For example, many of us belong to what we call 'Network Protocol Tribes.' These are specialized groups focused on certain fields. Weili, Sudair, and I are part of the 'Study Earthlings' Tribe. Since we're interested in researching Earth and its people, we work within this tribe, and that's how we can earn additional wealth."

I nodded, intrigued. "So, you're earning money just by studying me?"

"Exactly," Weili said with a smile. "We're currently working on building a physical research center where we'll display information and artifacts about Earth. Once it's completed, we'll earn more wealth. The more visitors we get — both virtually and in person — the more we continue to earn."

Sudair added, "On Guoke, most interactions happen in the virtual space. Our virtual visitors will be far more than those who come physically."

"We're planning to build the center right now," Norton said. "Let's head back to Weili's place so you can see how it's done."

Through the Global Movement Network, we quickly returned to Weili's home. Once we arrived, the three of them began working, their hands moving through the air as they interacted with holographic displays.

"How can you build something without going to the site?" I asked.

Weili smiled and gracefully turned her palm upward. "Everything's managed through the Global Information Network. We can complete the construction from here. Once it's done, we'll go check it out."

Norton explained further, "We first submitted a proposal to the 'Guoke Biology Research Protocol Tribe,' explaining why it's important to study Earth. Once it was approved, we earned the right to build our research center."

"And we've just paid the 'Guoke Construction Protocol Tribe' to help us build the structure," Sudair added. "But we need a blueprint, which can take some time."

"We don't need to make it from scratch," Weili said, already searching the Global Network. "I can find a pre-designed one."

Moments later, Weili announced the task was complete.

"So how long will it take them to build this research center?" I asked.

"A blink of an eye," Norton said. "It'll be finished in mere seconds by Earth's time."

"How can it be so fast?" I asked, still in disbelief.

"The construction tribe uses the Global Movement Network to cut, assemble, and transport materials with incredible speed," Norton explained. "Everything is automated, managed by the Information Network. Even the construction team doesn't physically go to the site. It's all done remotely."

Weili made a gesture, and suddenly, a large, intricate virtual grid expanded before us. Her hands moved gracefully as she declared, "The house is finished!"

We traveled to the site through the Movement Network, and there it was — a beautiful, towering structure, standing solidly in front of us. It was real, not virtual.

Norton ran his hand along the smooth wall, admiring the natural stone texture. "The material was cut directly from the mountain by the Movement Network. I love how the rock's natural pattern is preserved. It's beautiful."

"So, you'll earn a lot of money from this project?" I asked.

"Yes," Sudair confirmed, "our wealth value has increased. And as this research center grows in popularity, we'll keep earning more wealth over time."

"If it fails to attract people, though," Norton warned, "it might get demolished, and we won't earn anything more from it. In some cases, if a building turns out to be harmful or a waste, we might even lose wealth."

I scratched my head. "It seems like making money here is easy. Why did you say it's hard?"

"The challenge lies in getting approval and support," Norton explained. "You need to be part of a larger organization or 'tribe' to make money. It's almost impossible to succeed as an individual."

Weili nodded. "Individuals can offer personal services, engage in research, or create art to earn. You can even sell data from your intimate activities with a partner on the Global Information Network."

"Wait, what happens if you don't make any money at all?" I asked.

"You'll still be fine," Weili said, "as everyone receives regular wealth to cover basic needs. But if you want to enjoy a richer, more exciting life, you need to earn more."

"Besides," Sudair added, "if you just sit around hoarding wealth, not spending or contributing, the system will eventually deduct some of it. We don't encourage laziness on Guoke Planet."

Norton concluded, "Here, wealth is power. It gives you influence and the ability to control things, much like authority on Earth. The wealthier you are, the more power you have. In Guoke society, money is more than just currency—it's a tool for leadership."

Sudair laughed. "Also, on Guoke, most basic needs are free—nutrition, travel, housing, entertainment, healthcare, and even body replacement. It's only when you want something more that you must spend."

I smiled. "So, no chance of me taking any Guokean cash home to show off, huh?"

"Sorry," Sudair grinned. "Nothing from Guoke can leave the planet. That's the rule."

Chapter 27: Leadership on Guoke Planet

One day, I accompanied Norton, Sudair, and Weili to visit a renowned biologist on Guoke Planet named Aiwensen. He was similar in stature to Norton, with a composed demeanor, sharp eyes, and an air of wisdom. Aiwensen was not only Norton's colleague but also more famous — he was their leader.

Upon seeing me, Aiwensen said, "Welcome, Qian from Earth. I've always been intrigued by your planet. Like Norton, Weili, and Sudair, I'm a member of the 'Earth Study Tribe' on the Global Information Network. We frequently discuss Earthlings. Let's exchange some ideas."

Curious, I asked, "How many countries are there on Guoke Planet?"

"There is only one country — Guoke Planet itself," Aiwensen replied.

"So, who's the highest leader here?"

"We don't have a highest leader."

That threw me off. "No leader? Even criminal organizations on Earth have a boss. When I first arrived on your planet, I expected some big official to greet me, but no one did. Now I see why."

"Well, strictly speaking, the highest authority here is a virtual entity called the 'Global Information Network Algorithm Alliance,'" Aiwensen explained. "I am merely the head of the Biology Research Tribe, so I have authority in that field, but no further. Guoke's leadership isn't a person or even a group of people — it's a set of algorithms that everyone has agreed upon, developed over time. These algorithms govern us through the Global Information Network."

Nodding, I remarked, "On Earth, our leadership structure is like a pyramid. We have many countries, each with a leader, usually called a president or a prime minister. Below them are governors, mayors, and so on, until you reach ordinary citizens."

Norton chimed in, "On Guoke, the entire planet is one country, but it doesn't stop there. Our planet is part of a larger star system that includes dozens of inhabited planets, all governed by the same structure. There are no separate nations. Our leadership starts with the Global Information Network Algorithm Alliance, followed by tribe leaders like me, and then ordinary citizens."

Sudair interrupted, "In my opinion, the real power lies with those who control the Global Movement Network. Think about it — we depend on it for everything. In a way, it runs the whole planet."

"I disagree," Weili countered. "Our lives are governed by the wealth we earn, which is dictated by the 'Pricing Algorithm Tribe.' They decide how much our actions are worth, and that, I believe, is where the true power lies."

Norton nodded thoughtfully. "Assigning value to every action, in a world with so many people and so many tasks, is no small feat. The Pricing Algorithm Tribe was one of the first to form because people needed a way to fairly determine payment. Over time, these algorithms became so advanced that no individual could manage such complexity on their own."

Sudair then interjected with a personal story. "One time, I thought the Pricing Algorithm Tribe had shortchanged me on my wealth value. I threatened to file a complaint with the 'Global Information Network Supervision Alliance.' They immediately apologized and corrected the error. So, they didn't seem all that powerful to me. If anything, the tribes that directly distribute wealth seem more influential."

I laughed and said, "So after all that, even you all can't quite figure out who's truly in charge on your planet. It's like your leaders are just computer programs and virtual figures, not real people. How can you trust these virtual leaders to run your society? You're so advanced — how did this happen?"

Aiwensen smiled. "It wasn't something we planned overnight. As the Global Information and Movement Networks advanced, individual power became less important. People couldn't generate wealth without relying on these networks, and the networks solved most of our societal problems. Over time, virtual leadership became inevitable."

He waved his hand in the air, conjuring a holographic image. Scenes of ancient battles played out, with soldiers wielding primitive weapons in chaotic warfare. "In the past, Guoke Planet had many nations, much like Earth. Wars broke out constantly, mainly over resources—energy, wealth, and land. But when the Global Information and Movement Networks arrived, material wealth became trivial, almost free. With no need to fight over resources, and with currency fully digitized, governments lost their power. The state's role in defending its people, punishing crime, and maintaining order became redundant."

"As the state faded, the need for a traditional leader vanished too," Aiwensen continued. "In their place, the Algorithm Alliance took over. Our lives are now governed by mutually agreed-upon algorithms."

I hesitated before asking, "This might be a dumb question, but how hard is it to become a leader on your planet, like a tribe leader?"

"It's not easy," Aiwensen explained. "First, you need expertise in a specific area. Let's say you're an expert in biology and have innovative ideas. You would join the Biology Research Tribe and contribute regularly to discussions on the Global Network. Over time, if your contributions consistently surpass the current leader's, and that is reflected in the algorithms, you might replace them. However, it's a slow process. Remember, we live indefinitely, so patience is essential."

"Couldn't I just buy my way in?" I asked, half-joking. "If I had a lot of money, could I bribe my way to becoming a leader?"

Sudair laughed. "There's that Earthling love of bribery! You've always excelled at that."

Norton shook his head. "Bribery wouldn't work here. Most of our basic needs are free, so people aren't motivated by money the way they are on Earth. Besides, the Global Information Network Supervision Alliance would quickly catch any attempts to manipulate leadership roles with wealth."

Aiwensen added, "Earth has the internet, much like our Global Information Network. Once Earth deciphers the nature of fields, you'll be able to establish your own Global Movement Network. With that, countries will begin to fade, just as they did here, and eventually, Earth will be unified under one system."

I frowned. "So, in the end, who really holds the most power on Guoke?"

Aiwensen's answer surprised me. "The mathematicians. At the heart of it all, it's their algorithms that govern us. They control the digital world, and the digital world controls us. The true rulers of Guoke Planet are the ones who create and manage these algorithms."

"Not physicists?" I asked. "Isn't physics just as important?"

"Physics is crucial, but it has limits," Aiwensen explained. "Once a civilization fully understands the universe as a collection of objects and the space around them, with no mysterious third element, physics reaches its natural endpoint. It continues to develop, but only in breadth, not depth. Mathematics, however, has no end. Physics is just a branch of mathematics, describing the movement of objects through space."

Aiwensen's tone grew serious. "Mathematicians are formidable. They create algorithms that run everything, and they guard their knowledge carefully. Want to join their ranks? First, you must crack the codes they've set up. If you can't, you're locked out."

These "codes" were not just random obstacles — they were the foundation of their power. Algorithms were the language of leadership on Guoke Planet.

Chapter 28: Virtual Travel

One day, while lounging at Weili's home, I asked, "I've noticed something about the Guoke people — you all seem so relaxed, like nothing is urgent. Why is that?"

Weili, who was lying on her bed, rolled over and said, "That's because life on Guoke is mainly about leisure. Ordinary people aren't allowed to work, whether it's physical or mental labor. In fact, if regular people worked, they'd just mess things up. Everything here is run by the Global Movement Network and the Global Information Network, both of which are virtual and impossible to break. These networks are operated by artificial intelligence that has been perfected over thousands of years. No ordinary person could compete with it. Only those with special skills are allowed to work, and even they spend most of their time playing. If Earth's technology advances far enough, you'd see the same thing happen there."

She continued, "For most of us on Guoke, since the Global Movement Network automatically supplies our bodies with energy and nutrients, we don't need to worry about eating or drinking like you do on Earth. Our clothing is virtual, just a hologram projected onto us by the Global Information Network. Some of it is even grown from our bodies, so we don't have to worry about fashion either. We have no parents, no siblings, no sickness, and no fear of death. While Earthlings chase wealth and power, we chase experiences. Our entire lives are dedicated to play, and play gives us new experiences."

"I think I get it," I said. "But how do you play? Where do you go for fun, and what do you do?"

"Well, there are endless ways to have fun. We've already taken you to a few places. One of our favorite activities is virtual travel…" Weili paused, then suddenly leapt out of bed. "Qian, let me take you on a virtual trip!"

"Alright," I said, standing up and heading for the door. "Let's go then?"

"Where are you going?" she laughed, grabbing my arm and pulling me close. "We can do it right here."

Weili swiped her hand in the air, and a cloud of white smoke quickly turned into a three-dimensional image. It expanded, filling the room. The Global Movement Network and the Global Information Network had conjured a virtual scene right before our eyes.

A few large tree-like plants appeared, surrounded by vast grassland. Above us floated some Guoke script. The Global Information Network translated it for me as "The Wild Plains."

"We'll need to pick our gear — mounts, bows, weapons, even a servant or two. Oh, and we could also choose pets, though I think we can skip that. We're going to travel back to primitive times — think of it like Earth's Stone Age. Understand?" Weili asked, excited.

I nodded, though I didn't fully grasp what was happening. "Sure, I think I get it."

"Good. Let's begin our virtual journey." Weili swiped her hand again, and suddenly the room around us transformed. We were no longer in her home but standing on a vast, wild plain.

We were naked, except for a few leaves and flowers draped around us like primitive people. As we walked through the open field, Weili said she had chosen a setting reminiscent of Earth's early days.

Before long, we reached an area filled with various creatures. Each of us selected a mount that looked like a cross between a lion and a horse. In another location, we equipped ourselves with bows and curved blades. Despite her earlier decision to skip pets, Weili changed her mind, and we both picked small parrot-like birds to accompany us.

As we traveled, we came across three men chasing another man. Weili explained that the three were bandits hunting down a merchant and planning to kill him.

"We should help the merchant and fight the bandits," I suggested, but Weili wanted us to hide. "What happens if we lose the fight? Will it hurt?"

"No, not really. The virtual trip would just end," she replied nonchalantly.

"Then why not fight? Look, they've already killed the merchant."

"There's no reason. Just listen to me," Weili suddenly snapped. "I'll tell you when we can fight."

Later, when we encountered a larger group of enemies, Weili finally ordered us to attack. I hesitated, but Weili, swinging her blade wildly, charged in. We fought bravely, but our bodies were soon riddled with arrows. Each hit caused real pain, though it was mild compared to what it might feel like.

When it became clear we were about to be captured, we had no choice but to roll down a cliff to escape. At the bottom, I complained about Weili's reckless leadership, while she accused me of being a coward and an idiot. We argued until Weili, irritated, swiped her hand, ending the virtual trip and bringing us back to her home.

Weili, now playful again, looked at me coyly and said, "Qian, I was just teasing when I called you an idiot. You're not mad, are you? Shall we continue our virtual adventure?"

I shrugged. "I'm not mad. That felt so real—it's fascinating. I'd love to keep playing."

Weili's expression shifted suddenly. "But this time, we're traveling separately. I don't want to go with you anymore."

With another swipe of her hand, white smoke swirled up again, and soon we were back in a virtual landscape.

This time, I got to choose my own destination. I picked a place called the "Pink Blossom Garden." Why had Weili chosen such a violent place as the Wild Plains? I wanted something more peaceful, maybe even romantic. The description hinted at some exotic elements, and I wasn't disappointed.

The scene was serene — delicate pink silk scarves draped from the sky, and rows of peach trees lined the path ahead. Within each giant peach blossom was a beautiful woman with soft pink skin, posed seductively, trying to lure me in. A disembodied voice warned me, "Only by resisting temptation can you make it through."

As I walked, the blossoms grew closer and closer, brushing against me. The women inside exuded an intoxicating fragrance that made it hard to resist. Their soft skin invited me to stay, to lose myself in their embrace.

Just as I was about to give in and reach for one of the women, a heart-shaped balloon appeared between us, blocking my path. Guoke script flickered on the balloon, which the Global Information Network quickly translated: "Your beloved woman is calling you!"

Beloved woman? I sighed, guessing who it was. Sure enough, Weili appeared before me.

"I thought you didn't want to travel with me anymore?" I asked.

She smiled mischievously. "I changed my mind. Now, I want you to be my mount. I'll ride you wherever I go — from the Wild Plains to the ocean depths, you'll be my lion, my fish, my couch in a car, and my seat in a spaceship."

"I'm a person, not some mount," I protested.

"I can make you enjoy it," she replied confidently. With a wave of her hand, I transformed into a strange creature resembling a lion-horse hybrid. Weili climbed onto my back, pressing her bare skin against me, and I realized that perhaps being her mount wasn't so bad after all.

We traveled together once again, visiting primitive tribes, exploring the depths of the ocean, and even venturing into the fiery heart of a volcano. We saw many bizarre and wondrous places, but our destination was a war-torn planet where our spacecraft was shot down and destroyed.

Captured by the planet's inhabitants, we were dissected—our bodies cut open, each incision felt as real as if it were happening for real. I could even hear my skin being sliced.

Eventually, with the help of allies from other planets, we escaped and resumed our journey. But once again, Weili's poor leadership got us into trouble, and we ended our adventure bickering over who was to blame.

Still, Weili wasn't ready to stop. She invited Sudair and Norton to join us for a new adventure at a specialized virtual gaming arena.

The arena was massive and high-tech, with no doors—just circles on the ground beneath the walls. As we entered, standing in one of the circles, a glowing dot slowly spun around us. The walls displayed various Guoke scripts and images. Norton pressed something on the wall, and suddenly, we were inside.

The arena was divided into numerous sections, each designed for a different kind of game. Once inside, players would begin to float as if weightless, mimicking the sensation of zero gravity.

I soon realized that Guoke's virtual games used advanced field scanning technology to transmit signals directly into our brains, creating hyper-realistic sensations. Unlike at Weili's house, where the experience was more passive, this arena allowed for full immersion, with a wider variety of games and far more vivid scenes.

Though the pain felt from virtual injuries was real, it was muted compared to the actual experience. Yet, in erotic games, every sensation was indistinguishable from reality.

I played a few games — "Galactic Journey," "Battles with Savages," and "I Am King." Of course, the erotic-themed games were the most enticing and surreal.

In "Galactic Journey," I piloted a spaceship, flying through space and viewing different planets.

The voiceover provided detailed descriptions of inhabited planets, many of which boasted civilizations even more advanced than Guoke.

"Battles with Savages" took on a more Earth-centric theme. I noticed that Earthlings featured prominently, especially Americans, Europeans, Japanese, and Chinese.

Chapter 29: Experiencing Remote Sex

One day, I woke up from a nap to find that Weili was nowhere to be seen. I sat on the bed in a daze, when suddenly I heard soft music playing, and a cloud of white smoke began to rise beside me. Quickly, the smoke morphed into a 3D virtual image. Weili, wearing some sort of strange metallic outfit, appeared and spoke to me.

"Qian, I've left Guoke with Sudair and Norton. We're currently on a nearby planet and can't return for a while. Please don't wander outside my place — you could get hurt. If you're bored, you can play with this virtual console. Just point where you want to go, and it will take you there. Oh, and Qian, I miss you. I'll be back soon."

I played around with the virtual console for a bit. Weili's robot assistant even brought me food. As I studied the robot, which was constantly vibrating, I grew curious about what it was made of. When it got close to me, I impulsively grabbed it. The robot quickly dodged, but I still managed to catch it. As my hand went inside the robot's body, I felt a slight electric sensation on each of my fingers — it seemed even the robot's body was virtual.

Soon after, I watched as the robot transformed into a small red metallic liquid that flowed into a nearby box. I was beginning to feel like everything on Guoke was some kind of virtual reality. I tried to access the virtual travel feature on the console but struggled to navigate it. I ended up randomly pressing buttons, causing strange images and conversations between Guokeans and possibly other aliens to appear on the screen.

Later that night, I stopped fiddling with the console, and the 3D images vanished on their own. Lying in bed, I found myself daydreaming about the erotic scenes from the virtual sex games I'd seen before. I missed Weili and thought of her soft, seductive body.

Suddenly, the music started again, and a 3D image appeared beside me. Weili was in a metallic room, waving her hands at me from the screen.

"Qian, I'm currently staying in a spacecraft because there are no living accommodations on this desolate planet. I miss you — I want you to hold me," she said softly. "Look behind you at the red square on the wall. See that red dot in the center? Touch it."

I turned around and saw the red square. I pressed the red dot, and a box slid out. Inside was a soft, creamy white gelatinous substance that suddenly came to life, oozing onto the floor. Within seconds, it transformed into a perfect replica of Weili.

On the virtual screen, Weili continued to move and speak, and the white gelatinous figure mimicked her every movement and word exactly.

"Ah! Weili, you're back?" I asked.

"No, I'm not," both the virtual Weili and her clone said simultaneously.

Weili explained, "I'm transmitting my bodily signals to Guoke's Global Information Network, which then sends them to the red box in my home. The white gelatin in the box is activated by the signal and turns into a replica of me. This clone of me can receive all my movements and responses. Everything I do, the clone does too. If you have sex with it, the experience will be indistinguishable from being with me. It's the same in every way — there's no difference in sensation."

I approached the clone and hugged it. Indeed, it felt exactly like holding the real Weili. I even smelled her cleavage and down below—if anything, the scent was even more intense.

On the virtual screen, I saw Weili pull out a red box of her own. The gelatin inside quickly transformed into a clone of me. She embraced the clone tightly, just as my Weili-clone held onto me.

We rolled around on the bed, passionately making love. At one point, the Weili-clone instructed me to lie down while she straddled me.

"In Guoke, we engage in this kind of remote virtual sex far more often than actual physical sex," she explained.

"Why is that?" I asked.

"Because the clone's body can change shape," she replied. As if to prove it, the clone's soft white skin began shifting colors—gray, black, red, yellow, green, blue, and then back to white.

As she rode me, I watched her breasts lengthen until they were over a meter long, like flexible arms rubbing against me, feeling just like real breasts. Then she kissed me, her tongue extending deeper and deeper into my mouth, down my throat, and even into my stomach. I could feel her tongue's every movement as it slid along the insides of my body.

"I can release scents too," the clone said, and sure enough, I was enveloped by a rich, strange fragrance, like that of a young woman's perfume.

Her body transformed again, becoming smaller and slenderer, then taller and fuller. During our lovemaking, her body produced plenty of lubrication, though it never left her body to make a mess. After a while, I was completely drained of energy and fell asleep.

When I woke up, the Weili-clone was lying next to me in a frozen pose, expressionless. Glancing at the virtual console, I saw that Weili was busy with something in her spacecraft. She must have packed up the clone and red box on her end. I didn't know how to deactivate the clone, so I simply lay back down next to it and drifted off again.

The next time I woke up, the clone was gone, the virtual console had shut off, and the red box was back in place. I wasn't sure if Weili had turned it off remotely or if the system had deactivated itself, but I knew the remote sex session had ended.

The next morning, I was woken by the sound of Weili, Sudair, and Norton arriving home.

"How was the remote sex? Good, right?" Weili asked as she hugged me.

"Yeah, it was. But I'm completely exhausted."

"You took it too seriously!" Weili teased. "Did you make a mess?"

"No, of course not."

"I'll check," she said playfully. She pressed the red dot on the box, and it slid out. A portion of the white gelatin was stained yellow. "What's this? Qian, I think you made a mess."

Norton chuckled, "That's just Qian's semen. Earth men ejaculate during sex—it's different from us Guoke men. I'll need that for some experiments."

With a press on his earpiece, the yellow-stained part of the gelatin vanished—probably transported by the Global Movement Network.

"Earth men are messy," Weili said with mock disgust. "From now on, we'll stick to remote sex. That way, you won't dirty me."

Sudair laughed loudly. "Weili, our Guoke men are much cleaner, aren't they? Maybe we should develop a program on the Global Movement Network that specializes in cleaning up after Earth men!"

Weili, clearly amused, added, "You know what? I kind of like Qian's mess. Tonight, I'll make it my mission to get more of that white, sticky stuff from him—like the time before."

Sudair turned to Weili, teasing, "Did you record your remote sex session with Qian? If you did, you could upload it to the Global Information Network. You'd have thousands of Guoke men setting their virtual lovers to look like you! You'd be a sex star in no time."

"I'm not that special," Weili protested, "How would I become a star? Qian's just tall and big, which might attract some attention, but that's it."

"So, did you record it or not?" Sudair pressed.

"No, I didn't," Weili admitted, "But Norton probably did. He's been recording everything ever since he brought Qian from Earth. It's all part of his research."

Sure enough, Norton confirmed that he had not only recorded the remote sex but also captured our brain signals during the experience. The Guokeans loved turning their physical, mental, and even sexual experiences into data. They referred to these as "sex digits."

Some of them sold their sex digits on the Information Network, much like Earthlings selling albums or movies. This was a common and profitable business on Guoke. Of course, there were also many free sex digits available for fun. If a woman bought a man's sex digit, she could transform her information clay into a copy of him and experience sex with the digit, making it feel as real as the actual thing.

The Guokeans' real-time remote sex, like what Weili and I had done, was even more advanced—akin to a live broadcast. This allowed for fully synchronized experiences, though with one clear advantage: it was much easier to escape if things became uncomfortable. You could always terminate the connection.

Still, it wasn't without risks. If you weren't careful, you could accidentally set the energy level too high, and your partner might overwhelm you with their strength, stamina, and speed, leaving you exhausted and terrified. Some of the most popular sex digits had sold billions, turning their creators into full-fledged sex stars.

Eventually, Norton introduced me to some of these highly sought-after digits. There were men's, women's, and even gender-neutral digits. Some digits represented human-animal hybrids, while others were pure animal forms. When I tried out a few of these, I was blown away by how intense the experience was—there were no words to describe it. Even just a few minutes left an indelible mark on my mind, sending waves of pleasure through me.

When I shared my thoughts with Norton and the others, saying, "These amazing sex digits must cost a fortune, right?"

To my surprise, they responded that the best, most intense sex digits weren't even created by real people—they were generated by highly advanced artificial intelligence using powerful algorithms.

"On Earth," Norton explained, "anything artificial is often seen as inferior — something people avoid. Everyone chases 'all-natural' things. But here, it's the opposite. The sex digits of real people don't even come close to those created by AI. In terms of quality and sensation, the difference is like night and day."

He continued to explain that for the people of Guoke, sex digits were an essential part of life, not just an optional indulgence. "On Earth, people judge their romantic partners by looks or personality. Here on Guoke, what we care about in sex digits is uniqueness—novelty and individuality are what matter most. Quality isn't the primary concern."

Because of this, Norton said, they often travel to other planets and abduct beings from foreign worlds. Once brought to Guoke, these aliens produce sex digits that, while sometimes lacking in quality, are often popular for a period simply because they're exotic. If the experience proves to be good, and if it has a touch of the strange or mysterious, it can become a lasting trend, spreading even wider. The creator of such sex digits stands to gain immense wealth.

Chapter 30: The 3D Virtual Companions of Guoke Planet

On Earth, it's common for a boy to find a girlfriend or a girl to find a boyfriend as a companion. We're all familiar with this idea. Now, if a boy finds a girlfriend online just to chat with, we call that a "virtual companion."

However, on Guoke Planet, virtual companions have evolved on a massive scale, and their virtual companions are very different from what we know on Earth. The key difference lies in the incredible technological advances they possess.

The development of virtual companions on Guoke Planet went through five distinct stages, each shaped by the leaps and bounds of their technology.

Stage One: Communication through Devices

In the first stage, boys and girls communicated using physical devices like computers or phones, along with the global information network and dating software. They interacted through these tools, just as we do today on Earth. At this stage, Guoke Planet was not too different from where we are now, except their hardware and software were far more advanced.

Stage Two: Projection Tools for Realistic Interaction

The second stage introduced projection tools for interaction. Their phones and computers evolved to produce high-quality 3D projections, allowing people to create full 3D holographic images in their rooms. To achieve this effect, they installed several projection devices in different corners of the room. So, when they interacted through the global information network, it felt as if the other person was standing right there with them.

Earth has some basic projection technology, but the quality is still quite poor. Our images are rough, and the 3D realism is minimal. Some VR devices require users to wear special glasses, which is a major flaw. The people of Guoke Planet had already surpassed this stage.

Stage Three: Portable Holographic Interfaces

In the third stage, they used portable devices that created floating 3D virtual images. These devices were so small and discreet that they became almost invisible, leaving only the lifelike 3D images. A boy could see a beautiful girl standing before him, but it was just a tiny device projecting a virtual image of the girl.

At this stage, virtual companions looked incredibly realistic, could move around freely, and accompany their owners anywhere, blending seamlessly into various environments. However, the projection devices still had one flaw: they couldn't create an image if the light beam was blocked.

Stage Four: Pure Virtual Projection without Hardware

The fourth stage came with the invention of artificial field scanning technology, which revolutionized the concept of virtual companions. It eliminated the need for physical devices altogether. Artificial field scanning equipment could be installed in orbit, much like satellites, allowing them to remotely project 3D images and sound anywhere.

Unlike traditional projection, which used light beams to create images, artificial field scanning worked by collecting light at the location where the 3D image was to be displayed. It could even generate sound by vibrating the local air.

This technology had an incredible advantage: it could penetrate solid objects without interference. For instance, if you created a 3D virtual person outside and they walked into a building, the image wouldn't disappear. The artificial field scanning tech could project the image through walls without needing additional equipment inside the building.

By placing a few field scanning devices in space, they could generate 3D images and sound anywhere on the planet, making it accessible to all inhabitants. With this technology, interacting with virtual companions felt almost identical to living with a real partner. Even more impressively, these virtual companions could manipulate physical objects. For example, a girl could command her virtual boyfriend to move a table. Although the boyfriend was just a projection, the artificial field scanning tech would move the table, making it appear as if the virtual boyfriend had done it.

Stage Five: Interaction with "Information Clay" Avatars

The fifth and most advanced stage introduced "Information Clay." Imagine a boy entering a room and pressing a switch. Instantly, a 3D image of a beautiful girl from a distant location appears before him. The image moves towards a box, which automatically opens, revealing a substance called Information Clay.

As the image sinks into the box, the Information Clay comes to life, rapidly transforming into a physical replica of the girl. This replica is entirely controlled by the girl's remote actions, mimicking her every movement and gesture. The boy could interact with this Information Clay avatar, and the experience would feel identical to interacting with the real person.

Information Clay, made of particles as small as atoms, had no inherent power. Instead, its movement was powered remotely by the global transportation network. The signals controlling the Information Clay were handled by the global information network. This eliminated the need for each particle to have its own power source or communication system, making the technology both efficient and reliable.

With this technology, the boy could communicate and interact with the Information Clay avatar just like he would with a real person. He could even engage in physical activities, including sexual experiences, that felt indistinguishable from reality.

Weili once explained that some people on Guoke Planet who didn't have sexual organs used Information Clay to form tools for sexual activities. Their virtual holographic beings could also interact in this way, either with each other or with physical beings.

Sometimes, they didn't even need Information Clay. They could transmit sexual signals directly into the brain and experience purely virtual sex — a common and popular practice on Guoke Planet.

Chapter 31: The Sexual Arena

One day, Weili invited me to visit one of Guoke Planet's infamous sexual arenas, and I eagerly agreed. Weili explained that on Guoke Planet, there are many free public sexual arenas designed to satisfy the sexual needs of its inhabitants in various exotic environments. However, some private sexual arenas require participants to pay in wealth points.

Weili and I traveled through the global movement network to reach one of these public sexual arenas. It was enormous, stretching so far into the distance that I couldn't see its end. Above the arena, giant virtual letters floated in the air.

The arena's virtual spokesperson was a striking image: a woman straddling a man's neck. This was a classic pose on Guoke Planet, where women, whose bodies lack bones, could spread their lower bodies wide and envelop a man's entire head in a sudden leap.

The arena had no doors; its walls appeared to be made of solid material, with strange vertical grids filled with constantly shifting disturbances. At times, Guoke symbols would scroll upwards through the grids.

I saw many Guoke men and women entering the grids in pairs, but I also noticed a fair number of individuals going in alone.

"Why are there so many single people entering? How do they engage in sexual activities alone?" I asked.

Weili explained, "Once inside, singles can use the global information network to match with a sexual partner. If they can't find one, they can engage with virtual beings. The arena offers special equipment and environments that make the experience more intense than you could get from virtual sex at home."

Curious, I followed Weili to the walls of the arena, but as I hesitated, she pulled me forward and we entered the space.

Inside, it was just a narrow hallway with a giant 3D virtual image blocking our path. To the side stood a row of humanoid figures, each with a large hole where the face should have been.

I noticed some people sticking their heads into these face holes, so I did the same. Inside, I saw a scene of Guoke men and women engaging in sex. It wasn't particularly surprising—it was, after all, a sexual arena—but the sensual moans of the woman involved were so seductive that they hit me at my core, making me realize this place was far from ordinary.

Even after Weili pulled me away, those few seconds of moaning lingered in my mind, unforgettable. Later, I learned that most of these sounds were synthesized by artificial intelligence through complex algorithms. Some, however, were real but had been enhanced by the global information network for added effect. The voice of Kewen, our global information network assistant, had this kind of quality.

Weili pointed to a line of text on the virtual image and asked, "How about this one?"

The image showed a couple swinging naked on a swing set. "Too simple," I said.

"I thought so too," Weili replied and moved on to another suggestion. She pointed at an image where a naked person lay in the hollow of a horse-like animal while another woman rode the person's body as they drove the animal forward at high speed.

I wasn't particularly interested, but Weili loved the idea and, without waiting for my agreement, chose it.

In the blink of an eye, we found ourselves in a vast wilderness. Weili, naked, stood next to a horse-like creature, holding its reins.

"Where are we? What is this place?" I asked, confused.

"This is part of the sexual arena, but we're far from the main space. You can't access this area from anywhere else. Think of the main arena as just an entry point," Weili explained.

"But why can't you get here from outside? What's so special about this place?"

"Enough questions," Weili said, her tone suddenly firm. "Come over here and lie in this."

I did as she instructed, lying inside the hollow of the creature, and Weili straddled me, her body pressing down as she guided the animal into a gallop.

At first, it was thrilling. But soon, the rough jumps across ravines and hard landings made Weili slam into me painfully. She was ecstatic, though, and ignored my requests to stop. Only after some time did she finally relent, smiling, and said, "We haven't even done the fun parts yet — jumping over fire, climbing stairs, crossing rivers…"

"No more," I protested. "Let's switch. You lie in here, and I'll ride on top."

Uninterested in being the rider, Weili swiftly moved on to the next activity, pulling up a virtual interface. The next scenario she chose showed a couple enclosed in a large transparent sphere, rolling downhill like a giant bowling ball.

"Let's try this," I suggested, but Weili seemed hesitant.

"We've done this one before," she said.

"This time, we'll do it differently," I insisted. "I'll be more prepared."

Reluctantly, she agreed. We soon found ourselves locked inside the large, soft sphere, naked and holding each other tight as it began rolling down a hill. Transparent liquid dripped onto our skin, forming the sphere around us. The material was soft yet firm, making it easy to move while maintaining an intimate embrace.

As we rolled down the hill, bouncing over rocks and crashing into obstacles, the sensation was electrifying. We hit jagged stones, causing the sphere to bounce into the air, making Weili scream with excitement. The experience was exhilarating and slightly terrifying, but it left us breathless with adrenaline.

After a few minutes, the sphere dissolved into a puddle, and we were back on solid ground. Weili, ever the thrill-seeker, began searching for another game. Our next adventure involved traveling inside a human body model, and Weili insisted on using an Earth-based one.

Naked and entwined, we jumped down the throat of the giant body, sliding down its esophagus, and eventually entered its stomach. The body was alive and constantly moving, giving us the sensation of being pushed and squeezed by soft, pulsating muscles.

Eventually, we made our way through the intestines and out through the rectum, coated in a sticky, viscous substance. As the liquid dried, it flaked off, leaving us clean once more.

Exhausted yet exhilarated from the endless string of bizarre sexual games, I finally suggested we return home, but Weili wasn't ready to stop. She proposed one final game that promised to restore my energy. In a matter of seconds, I was enveloped by a soft, virtual cocoon that put me into a deep, restful sleep. When I awoke, feeling completely revitalized, I asked Weili how it worked.

"This is a combination of the global movement and information networks at work. They can create a state of complete relaxation for both the mind and body," she explained.

Despite my suggestion for her to try it, Weili said she didn't need the rest, and so our adventures continued into the night.

Chapter 32: Encounter with the Electric Girl and the Snake Girl

One day, Weili, Sudair, and I were invited by Norton to a private venue — a place only accessible by special invitation. Weili swiped her hand in the air, activating Guoke Planet's global movement and information networks. A virtual screen appeared next to her, displaying her figure. She examined her body from the front and back, showing how much she cared about this gathering.

We used the global movement network to appear outside the private venue and met up with Norton and Sudair. Their outfits were even more revealing than usual—short, minimal, and daring.

Norton touched his ear briefly, and suddenly, we were transported inside the venue. The owner must have granted Norton's request to enter. Inside, the place was packed with people. Dim, low music filled the air, and everyone's bodies were nearly fully exposed. Some wore virtual garments so small that many appeared completely naked. Their skin shimmered, resembling polished metal, glowing in various bright colors under the intermittent flashes of white light.

Weili, Norton, and Sudair each received a small glowing stick, which they slowly inserted into their arms. The stick's tip emitted rings of blue and silver light, giving their faces an eerie, ghostly look.

Weili told me, "Qian, you can't use this. Your body is different from ours. I'll get you something else." She returned with some metallic, glowing liquid and rubbed it on my hands and shoulders.

Under the dark light, my skin began to glow faintly blue, though not as intensely as theirs.

They also received cups filled not with drinks but with blue vapor, which they would inhale from time to time. Weili explained to me that the vapor was a hallucinogen, meant to heighten excitement and alter moods. "But you Earthlings can't use it," she warned.

Norton asked Weili to keep an eye on me, and soon after, he and Sudair disappeared. Weili was in high spirits, leading me through the crowd. At one point, she asked me to wait while she stepped away, promising to return soon.

As I stood there alone, two Guoke women noticed me. They were arm-in-arm, one with a device playing loud, rhythmic, and grating electronic music. As they stopped in front of me, one woman, unable to stop herself, swung around the other due to momentum, and they both turned their attention to me. They whispered to each other, and I heard their conversation through the global information network assistant, Kewen:

"He's huge! An alien, clearly."

"A big guy, obviously a man."

"Let's grab him, take him back, and violate him. Get inside him. It'll be a new experience."

"I love new, exciting experiences..."

"We can't let this opportunity slip by."

The first woman, who was petite, stood about a meter tall with a tiny waist that was no wider than my arm. She wore a short skirt and was bare-chested, her small, long breasts tied together with a ribbon. Her jet-black, metallic hair, smooth and shiny, hung in pipe-like strands with white, ring-like markings. She had the appearance of a snake—her limbs and torso slithering and twisting with a boneless fluidity.

Her body glowed an opalescent blue, smooth and glossy like polished jade. Her eyes were large and narrow, so long that they extended beyond the sides of her face at a 45-degree angle, glowing an intense blood-red.

As she approached, her mouth suddenly stretched wide, revealing rows of thin, fleshy tubes that writhed inside like frenzied worms. She looked like a living nightmare. She pressed a finger to her ear and said something to her companion. Kewen translated: "Request for global movement network assistance to relocate the target denied."

The snake woman had tried to use the movement network to abduct me but failed. She edged closer, seemingly ready to try physically taking me herself.

Kewen's urgent warning rang out: "Danger. Intent to sexually assault. Advise immediate retreat."

I hesitated, concerned that if I moved, Weili might not find me. The woman drew nearer, and Kewen's warning grew louder: "Leave now. Imminent risk of mechanical assault."

Despite the warnings, I remained in place. Her appearance, while terrifying, was also captivating. Her shimmering body and serpentine curves were alluring. I had been playing so many virtual sex and combat games lately that I thought there couldn't be any real danger.

But as the snake woman moved to embrace me, a sharp, pungent odor — like rotting insects —

wafted from her body. It triggered a primal disgust, and I instinctively stepped back, avoiding her touch.

At that moment, the second woman approached. She had disheveled hair, a fuller figure, and oversized thighs. Her enormous breasts contrasted sharply with her tiny hands and feet. Kewen's voice returned: "Electric Girl, intent to sexually assault. Possible danger: electrical burns."

Before I could react, Electric Girl grabbed me from behind, and a jolt of electricity surged through my body. My limbs froze, unresponsive.

In that moment, Snake Girl jumped onto me, wrapping her legs around my waist with the speed of a frog. Her virtual clothing vanished, and her skin, smooth and cool like a wet eel, pressed against me.

I felt her body slide down as I became enveloped in her soft, slippery embrace. My lower body sank into her, and a powerful suction pulled me deeper. Her thin, long breasts wrapped around my waist like arms. I felt a wave of pleasure unlike anything I had ever experienced, intensified by the electric shocks from behind.

For a moment, I thought, *this is pure ecstasy. Who needs to listen to Kewen's warnings when I could have missed this?*

But soon, I realized something was wrong. A soft tube slipped into my anus, and with my arms and waist firmly bound by her writhing body, I couldn't see what was happening behind me. Kewen's display in my mind showed a confusing image of the three of us entangled, but it was unclear what was invading my body.

Despite my best mental efforts to resist, the tube continued to push inside, filling me with a strange sense of pleasure mixed with growing fear.

Snake Girl kissed me, and her mouth flooded with thin, foul-smelling tubes that slithered into my throat and down into my stomach. The tube in my anus pushed further, twisting inside, wrapping around my organs. I felt like I was being trapped from the inside out.

A strange combination of arousal and disgust overwhelmed me, but I couldn't fight it. When I opened my eyes, I saw Snake Girl's body shrinking as she pushed more of herself into me. Soon, I was bloated, filled with her writhing presence.

Electric Girl's body released hundreds of thin, worm-like tendrils that crawled over my body, searching for entry points. Some tried to force their way through my navel.

Just when I thought the ecstasy couldn't become any more intense, a booming voice cut through the chaos: "Let him go immediately!"

Norton and Sudair had arrived. Electric Girl released her grip and fled instantly. Without her support, I could barely stand, my body now weighed down by Snake Girl, who was still partly inside me.

Snake Girl, in a panic, began pulling herself out. I felt her tubes withdraw from my throat and anus, leaving a painful burning sensation. She reassembled herself on the floor, her body once again smooth and shining like jade, before darting off into the shadows.

I collapsed, feeling a searing pain spread through my body. Blood trickled down my legs. The hasty withdrawal had injured me.

Norton immediately contacted Weili, who arrived in a state of shock, horrified by the sight of my injuries. Her appearance had changed drastically—her face was now stretched and dog-like, with large, pointed ears and snake-like hair. The sight of her reminded me of a nightmare, a far cry from the romantic fantasies I'd had of bringing her back to Earth to be my wife.

Despite my pain, I felt a sudden urge to lash out, but I couldn't even stand. Norton and Weili decided to end the gathering and take me to a Guoke hospital for treatment.

The hospital was massive, with few people inside. Its virtual spokesperson, a cute little girl, floated in the air, greeting us. A giant cylindrical device, large enough to fit a small house, stood in the center of the room.

Weili supported me as I stumbled forward. "This is the Artificial Information Field Scanner," she explained. "It can heal any injury, even those you Earthlings suffer from. All you need to do is lie inside, and it will fix everything."

I stepped inside, and within seconds, a faint electrical current washed over me, making me feel a slight tingling sensation as it moved through my body from head to toe. Just seconds later, the pain and discomfort vanished.

The machine had healed me entirely. I was stunned by its effectiveness as we returned to Weili's home.

"Artificial Information Fields can heal anything," Weili boasted. "With one of these machines, Earth's women would never need another beauty product. They could sculpt their bodies however they wanted."

Norton, ever the scientist, added, "When Earth figures out the true nature of fields, you'll be able to create these machines too. Then, diseases like cancer, diabetes, and even mental illness will be a thing of the past."

The technology was miraculous, and as I sat recovering in Weili's home, I couldn't stop thinking about how different the world would be if Earth had this kind of power.

Chapter 33: Visiting Neighboring Planets

While talking with Norton and the others, I learned that there are dozens of planets near Guoke Planet, much like the eight planets revolving around our sun on Earth. Some of these planets even have satellites—some of the larger planets have dozens of moons. Guoke civilization began on one of these planets, and only after they invented faster-than-light spacecraft did they start developing the surrounding planets on a large scale.

Most of the neighboring planets of Guoke have been developed and are now habitable. Some even have a significant population. Once, Norton, Sudair, Weili, and I boarded a spacecraft to tour a few of these planets.

Our first stop was the Garbage Planet. This planet is filled with heaps of trash, its thin atmosphere unsuitable for breathing. The spacecraft hovered above the Garbage Planet while Norton and Sudair disembarked, leaving Weili and me aboard.

Weili explained, "Our planet has extremely strict environmental regulations, so much of our waste, especially decommissioned spacecraft, is transported here for decomposition. After processing, the reusable materials are sent back to us."

Most of the labor on the Garbage Planet is done by robots, which are controlled remotely by people back on Guoke Planet.

Our second stop was a massive planet where the spacecraft circled above endless rows of towering metallic structures. The planet gleamed silver-white but still looked barren. There were no plants—at least, I saw none despite my efforts to find any.

"This is our home planet, Silver Star," Norton explained, which surprised me. "Guoke people originated here. It used to be like Earth, full of greenery and life, but centuries of nuclear war nearly destroyed it — over a hundred years of war by Earth's reckoning. The surface became uninhabitable, forcing us to live underground."

Fortunately, not long after, they decoded the true nature of fields and invented spacecraft. Their first mission was to develop Guoke Planet, where they transformed the environment to suit human habitation. Now, Guoke is their primary planet — the center of power and technology, governing the other planets.

"Most of the inhabitants of Silver Star today are virtual beings or people who live permanently underground," Norton continued.

Our spacecraft entered Silver Star through a tunnel. As we descended, Norton handed me a collar, explaining that the underground air might not be suitable for humans. The collar blocked air from entering my nose and mouth, while the spacecraft's artificial field scanner transferred oxygen directly into my bloodstream.

We disembarked and switched to another form of transportation, similar to an open-top car but without wheels, floating about two meters off the ground at a leisurely pace. It was perfect for sightseeing. The interior of Silver Star resembled a giant centipede, with a vast central tunnel and numerous smaller tunnels branching off. Apparently, there were multiple layers of tunnels beneath the main one.

We occasionally saw vast underground spaces filled with vibrant green and yellow plants, as if bathed in sunlight. However, the cramped environment felt oppressive, lacking the open skies and fresh air that make life on Earth so free.

As we continued, we passed walls filled with virtual people walking back and forth. Sometimes, light-based virtual beings would walk straight through us, a jarring yet fascinating experience. In the dim light, strange reptilian creatures scurried into smaller tunnels as we approached.

After leaving Silver Star, we flew to the Primitive Tribe Planet. Norton explained, "Most of the residents of this planet are immigrants from Guoke Planet. There's a forum on the global information network called 'I Am Primitive Tribe,' which acts as the central authority for this planet. They reject technology, yet ironically rely on some basic technological products. The forum played a key role in developing this planet."

The surface of the Primitive Tribe Planet was lush and beautiful, covered in greenery. Sudair piloted the spacecraft at low altitudes, skimming the treetops.

"Be careful," Norton warned. "The people here like to attack others. They hate technology and laws, and they glorify violence and the law of the jungle. It's common for them to kill one another."

Sure enough, we saw human remains exposed on the ground, adding a gruesome contrast to the planet's natural beauty. The skeletons were stark and unsettling.

Norton explained, "The bodies of 'I Am Primitive Tribe' members were custom-made on Guoke Planet. They have bones and need to eat food, unlike us. Our nutrition is provided automatically by the artificial field, controlled by the global movement network. But on this planet, there is no artificial field or global network. They have to eat to survive, just like Earthlings."

The inhabitants of the Primitive Tribe Planet were varied in appearance — some were fat, others thin, and their heights and looks were all over the place. Their clothes were tattered, and nearly everyone carried weapons ranging from simple blades and bows to firearms and more advanced arms I couldn't name.

"What happens when these people die?" I asked, intrigued.

"Their consciousness is backed up on Guoke Planet. When they die, they're resurrected there, but they lose their memories of life on the Primitive Tribe Planet. The 'I Am Primitive Tribe' forum on Guoke Planet has satellites monitoring the planet. They know instantly when someone dies, and they resurrect them on Guoke if they want to return."

Sudair sneered. "It's a miserable existence on that planet. No technology, no global network, and always worrying about food. I don't understand why anyone would choose to live there."

Weili chimed in, "It's because they're obsessed with killing real people, not just virtual enemies. There's no other place where they can do that freely."

"Only to get killed themselves!" Sudair laughed.

Next, we visited the Flower Planet, a paradise of strange and beautiful plants, a literal sea of flowers. The air was sweet with fragrance as we wandered through the fields. They had me stand alone in a patch of red flowers to take a picture, though I didn't see them use a camera. They probably had a more advanced way of capturing images.

"These red flowers were brought from Earth. Do you know what they're called?" Norton asked.

"No, but I've seen them before at home," I admitted.

"They're called crepe myrtles on Earth," Norton said. "Many Guoke people come here to relax. It's a great spot."

"But stay too long, and it becomes boring," Sudair added.

Weili nodded in agreement.

Our spacecraft then approached a small, distant planet. Sudair hovered the craft above its surface without landing. Norton explained, "This planet is the farthest from the central star of the Guoke system and serves as our early warning center, monitoring visitors from other solar systems."

The buildings on the planet were peculiar, stretching horizontally across the surface. I figured the planet's low gravity allowed for such structures, which would otherwise collapse under normal gravitational forces.

We visited another planet where an enormous, crashed spacecraft lay buried under thick dust. Sudair steered closer, activating the scanners to get a view inside. The scanner revealed skeletons within the wreckage.

"These were some of our early explorers," Norton said solemnly. "Back then, we hadn't yet developed the ability to back up our consciousness.

When these pioneers died, they were gone for good. They were true heroes."

On another desolate planet, we found remnants of early colonization efforts. Norton explained that this was one of their failed attempts to terraform a small planet. They had thought smaller planets would be easier to modify, but they discovered it was difficult to retain an atmosphere. When the artificial field maintaining the atmosphere malfunctioned, the air escaped, resulting in disaster.

Indeed, we saw houses filled with skeletons embracing each other, a chilling reminder of the failed colonization. Norton said, "When the atmosphere disappeared, many couples chose to die in each other's arms. Early Guoke exploration was fraught with danger."

Our next destination was the Mining Planet, an enormous body that was once the primary source of minerals for Guoke. However, as technology advanced, Guoke developed the ability to transform materials at a molecular level, making resources like gold and diamonds as common as dirt. Mining was no longer necessary, and the planet became deserted.

The Mining Planet had many moons, some as large as Earth. Many of these moons had been developed or were being developed for habitation.

Finally, we visited the Lovers' Twin Planets, a pair of celestial bodies orbiting around each other while also revolving around their star, the sun of the Guoke system.

"Lovers' Twin Planets used to be called Sisters' Twin Planets," Weili explained, "but once we achieved immortality and the ability to clone ourselves, the concept of siblings faded away. Now they're called Lovers' Planets. One planet is black, the other white, so they're also known as the Black and White Twins. People refer to the black one as the male planet and the white one as the female planet."

From our vantage point on the black planet, the white planet appeared massive, hovering ominously overhead, slowly moving across the sky.

Norton said, "The two planets orbit each other more quickly than your Earth's moon orbits your planet."

Sudair remarked, "Even though these planets are being heavily advertised as romantic getaways, few people want to live here. The conditions are too harsh—day and night cycles are unpredictable, and the weather is strange due to the twin planets blocking each other's sunlight. It's not exactly paradise."

We flew past the surface of the white planet, seeing the massive black planet looming above like a shadow. I noticed that the black planet's surface had many peaks and valleys, which might explain its dark appearance.

Our final visit was to one of the system's industrial planets. It was filled with towering metal buildings and countless factories. Norton explained that there was no atmosphere here and that robots performed all the work, controlled remotely by Guoke people.

After visiting the industrial planet, we returned to Guoke, having only scratched the surface of what their planetary system had to offer.

Chapter 34: Abducted on Mercury

Near Guoke Planet lies a massive planet almost entirely covered by water, known as "Mercury" by Norton and the others. One day, Norton, Sudair, Weili, and I took a spacecraft to visit and explore Mercury.

The spacecraft reached Mercury instantly from Guoke Planet and hovered above the planet's surface, as Norton and Sudair seemed to be selecting a landing spot. Based on the visual information provided by the global information network, the spacecraft appeared to descend slowly. However, as we approached the water, I could still feel the rapid plunge into the sea. When the spacecraft entered the water, it created no splashes, as if it had silently turned into a puff of smoke — quite a mystical sight.

Underwater, the spacecraft's large 3D projection screen provided a panoramic view of the surrounding scenery. The speed of the spacecraft slowed, allowing us to take in the dense, towering plants and a wide array of fish swimming around. Norton pointed to a creature resembling a shark and said, "This fish is not just any ordinary species. Inside its belly resides a highly intelligent humanoid, part of a water-based parasitic species brought in from another planet in the universe. Look closely; the human-like intelligence is visible in its eyes, entirely different from other fish."

Weili added, "We've encountered these fish before while playing in the oceans of Guoke Planet. If they catch you, it would be a disaster."

I asked, "Are the inhabitants of Mercury from Guoke Planet, or did they evolve here?"

Norton replied, "Mercury initially hosted only low-level virus-like organisms but never evolved intelligent life. Once we developed faster-than-light spacecraft, Guoke explorers frequently visited nearby planets, and Mercury became well-known. The 'I Am Mercury' group on the global information network made great efforts to introduce various species, some kidnapped from distant planets in the universe, especially the water-based parasitic species. After modifying them, they released them into Mercury's waters. Some even altered their own bodies to live inside large fish, spending their entire lives in the watery depths of Mercury."

Sudair commented, "The translations you're hearing now rely on our spacecraft's equipment. Mercury has no global movement or information network, so living here is beyond miserable. I can't understand why anyone would willingly live in these conditions."

Weili added, "The 'I Am Mercury' forum on the global information network often discusses how Mercury's vast oceans are sparsely populated, and the lack of partners is the biggest problem. Although they can invite others from Guoke Planet to join them underwater, few respond. There are more women than men underwater here, and these women are especially interested in male tourists from Guoke. If they catch you, you'll be reduced to a sex slave."

I looked out of the spacecraft's 3D screen and saw a few shark-like fish slowly trailing us. Norton cautioned Sudair to be careful, but Sudair dismissed his concerns, "What can these fish possibly do to us?"

Norton responded, "These underwater beings have lived here for thousands of years. They've evolved into highly intelligent creatures. If something goes wrong, our bodies and consciousness are backed up on Guoke, so we're safe. But 'Qian' doesn't have that luxury—he could die permanently. Weili's right: these beings are cunning, so we should remain vigilant."

"You're right," Sudair agreed. "I'll fly carefully and avoid risky areas."

Curious, I asked, "How do these underwater beings communicate with the 'I Am Mercury' forum on Guoke? How do they send information to the global information network?"

Norton explained, "They used to record their information, which members of the 'I Am Mercury' group would retrieve by spacecraft and upload to the global information network. But now, according to the forum, they've solved the problem of instant communication. Many of the underwater beings' bodies are now wirelessly connected to Guoke's global network."

We spent a long time exploring underwater. Norton suggested, "There's a small island nearby. Let's check it out. Qian, wear this around your neck—it will allow our spacecraft to provide you with oxygen since you can't breathe Mercury's air."

Weili handed me a half-circle collar, which likely prevented me from inhaling the planet's atmosphere. Sudair piloted the spacecraft out of the water and into the sky. Soon, we spotted the small island.

The island was small and low, with hardly any plants. It seemed like it had been frequently flooded by seawater. The soil resembled a white clay-like substance, mostly pale gray.

Norton explained, "This island's soil contains a high amount of water-soluble material, which is why Mercury has so little land. Most of the landmass has been dissolved by the sea."

While I wandered near the edge of the island, Weili warned me, "Stay away from the water, Qian. If one of those fish swallows you, you'll become their sex slave, and we won't be able to save you."

Her warning frightened me, and I quickly stepped away from the shoreline. I noticed several large holes on the island, filled with water, with their edges looking churned, as if frequently disturbed by something moving in and out.

"What caused these holes?" I asked. "They look like holes eels dig, but much larger."

"We're not sure," Sudair answered. "It's likely some large creature."

"It doesn't look volcanic," Norton added. "It's probably from a large animal burrowing."

As I crouched to inspect one of the larger holes, the water inside suddenly receded, and the ground beneath me collapsed. I tumbled into the hole and was quickly pulled deeper by a powerful suction. Before I could call for help, I slid through the muddy tunnel, which connected to the sea. I saw a massive fish with its mouth wide open, waiting for me.

As I approached the fish's mouth, the white clay washed off my body, and my virtual clothing disappeared, leaving me completely naked. The fish stopped sucking in water, but my momentum carried me straight into its belly, where a hole in its stomach sucked me inside. The hole was tight, but the force was too strong to resist.

Inside the fish, it was warm compared to the cold seawater, and I found it hard to breathe. Suddenly, a soft tube attached itself to my head, expanding and allowing me to breathe again. However, I continued sliding deeper into the fish's body, coldness once again gripping me.

Eventually, I stopped moving and heard strange music, unlike anything I had ever encountered. The fish's stomach was illuminated with a faint blue glow, resembling soft fluorescent light. I could see through the transparent tube covering my head. In front of me sat a strange, seductive woman, small in stature, and completely naked. Could this be the high-level underwater being Weili had warned me about? I'd been captured! Would I ever return?

The woman had white, translucent skin with a hint of green, looking like jade or jelly, and appeared to have no bones. Her small, pointed breasts jutted out like horns. Her black, glossy hair clung to her head like the sleek back of a fish, trailing behind her. Her eyes were large, her nose and mouth tiny, and her face was smooth and featureless except for the upward curve of her eyes, which gave her a seductive, sinister look. She was connected to the fish's body by a thick tube attached to her back.

Her small stature—no more than 70 or 80 centimeters tall—and her smooth, delicate features gave her an appearance both alluring and eerie. However, her eyes held the same look of desire I had seen in women on both Earth and Guoke Planet.

This woman was speaking, but I couldn't understand a word. Without the global information network translating for me, I was truly stranded. What was I to do? Could I overpower her and demand my release? But as I approached her, drawn by her smile or perhaps her lascivious gaze, I reached out to grab her throat. The moment I touched her, a jolt of electricity surged through me, darkening the surrounding light.

I collapsed onto my back from the shock, while the woman swiftly jumped on top of me, straddling my chest with her legs apart. Her skin felt as smooth and slippery as a wet eel.

Her crotch was directly above me, and I saw it suddenly split open, revealing numerous green tubes of varying lengths and thicknesses. These tubes, which looked soft, had pale blue and reddish-purple tips, contrasting with the green exteriors.

The tubes twisted and writhed like a nest of snakes, eager to lash out and seize something. Suddenly, a thick green fluid sprayed out from the tubes, coating my entire body. It felt warm, and almost immediately, I was overcome with a surge of energy, as if I had been injected with a potent stimulant.

She pressed her crotch firmly against my chest, then slowly slid her body backward, moving to my waist, and then further down. My penis entered her, and the soft tubes inside her wrapped around me, tightening and bringing waves of intense pleasure.

As her eyes leaked a clear fluid that dripped onto my chest and absorbed into my skin, a massive burst of energy coursed through my entire body. The pleasure was so intense that it became overwhelming, almost unbearable, but soon I felt sleep overtaking me.

At some point, I felt a tube entering my anus, instantly shaking off the sleepiness in a wave of fear. I tried to resist mentally, to stop it from penetrating me, but it was no use. Sleep began to wash over me again, and as I succumbed, the tube continued to slowly work its way deeper inside.

Inside me, the tube continued to pump warm, thick liquid, filling me with inexhaustible energy. Gradually, the tube climbed through my intestines, all the way up to my stomach, and finally stopped at my throat.

When I woke up, the transparent tube that had covered my head was gone, and the woman had moved off me, though a thick green tube still connected her to me through my anus.

Suddenly, I felt something strange in my mouth. I opened it to find, to my horror, a green snake-like tube emerging. I looked down and saw that the same thing was happening to my penis, with a thin green tube extending from it.

Seeing me awake, the woman grew excited, spreading her legs again as more of her tubes extended, writhing in the air before attaching themselves to my body. Countless tubes latched onto me, sucking and caressing me inside and out, like hundreds of gentle hands massaging me, sending indescribable waves of pleasure through my entire body.

The tubes once again sprayed their warm, sticky liquid, and I closed my eyes, feeling the ecstasy reach its peak. Just then, a sudden force shoved me, and before I knew it, I was tossed out of the fish's body.

In the clear seawater, I could still see the green tube trailing from my anus. The sticky green fluid spread around me in the water, and the cold of the ocean felt like a thousand needles piercing my skin. It was painful.

Strangely, I didn't need to breathe and felt no discomfort. My skin was freezing, but inside, I felt warm. I guessed the tube attached to my anus was providing me with some kind of energy.

I tried to struggle, but the tube yanked at my organs painfully. Why had that woman thrown me out of the fish's body? Was she trying to cause me more pain?

It suddenly dawned on me that I had become her slave. Would I ever see Norton or Weili again? Would I ever return to Earth and reunite with my parents? A deep sadness washed over me.

As the cold water became unbearable, I curled up. Suddenly, the tube tugged at me again, sending searing pain through my insides, and I was slowly pulled back into the fish's body.

The demonic, snake-like woman sat inside the fish's stomach, waving her hands at me and speaking, but I couldn't understand a word she said.

After she injected me with another liquid, my brain filled with green, and I instantly fell asleep. When she sprayed a different liquid, my brain flashed red, and I was jolted awake, full of manic energy.

Most of the time, I remained in a deep slumber, only to be awakened when she needed me for sex. Eventually, the tube connected to my anus grew up my spine and reached my brain, allowing me to communicate with her telepathically. When I closed my eyes, I could even see the ocean around me, though my vision was blurry and limited.

As Weili had predicted, the woman treated me as nothing more than her slave. Had she altered my body in some way? My skin had changed color, taking on a greenish hue. I didn't know exactly what she had done with her tubes inside me, but the thought filled me with fear and anxiety.

Now that we could communicate, and I could vaguely perceive the underwater world, I felt somewhat calmer. The desperate urge to escape and reunite with Norton and the others slowly faded.

I even began to enjoy holding this tiny woman in my arms as we roamed the ocean, a part of me growing attached to her. But my reprieve didn't last long.

A violent jolt woke me, sending waves of pain through my organs. I opened my eyes to see the woman convulsing beside me, her body trembling uncontrollably, and the green tube connecting us had been severed.

The scene around me had changed. We were no longer underwater, but inside a large spacecraft. The fish's body lay dissected before us, with several robots working on it.

After a while, the fish's remains were tossed back into the ocean, and I watched on the virtual display as its body made a huge splash in the water below.

I saw Norton pacing back and forth, talking to someone through the global information network. A sudden realization hit me: this entire ordeal had likely been part of an experiment orchestrated by Norton.

Several robots approached, placing both me and the unfortunate woman into separate containers.

Later, in a hospital on Guoke Planet, I met Norton, Weili, and Sudair. Norton said, "Apologies. Due to our negligence, you ended up in a dangerous situation."

"Weili asked, 'How are you feeling?'"

"Dizzy, weak, and nauseous," I replied.

"Don't worry, a few sessions with the artificial information field will fix you right up," Sudair reassured me.

I lay in the artificial field scanner, and after a while, I felt much better.

Norton pointed at the virtual display and said, "Look, we removed all these strange substances from his body. These are from the parasitic sea creatures. His body is still altered, though, and the artificial field alone won't fix it. We'll need to use the plant-based therapy to fully cure him."

At the plant therapy hospital, I was led to a large tank, and Norton and the others controlled everything remotely through the virtual screen. The top of the tank opened, revealing writhing red tubes inside, their ends like gaping maws.

Cursing Norton in my mind, I was helpless as I dropped into the tank. Instead of crashing onto the tubes, I was gently held and wrapped up, the tubes caressing me, filling me with a soothing sensation.

Later, I felt the liquid filling the tank, enveloping me completely, but I could still breathe comfortably, likely due to the tube providing me with oxygen.

Finally, after completing the plant-based therapy, I felt fully recovered.

Chapter 35: A Gift for the Amphibious Giants

When I reunited with Norton, Sudair, and Weili, they began discussing the parasitic species living in the ocean depths of Mercury. Norton explained that on Guoke Planet, there are also various parasitic species, including an amphibious race. These beings were originally brought from a highly advanced planet and can live both underwater and on land.

Their home planet is incredibly developed, with large, sophisticated buildings and advanced technology. In their early days, they were solitary beings, but eventually, they developed the ability to manufacture their own bodies, leading them to form communities. As one of the highest forms of intelligence in the universe, their males are small and usually live parasitically inside female bodies.

Norton waved his hand, and a three-dimensional hologram appeared, displaying the body of a female that resembled a human woman. He explained that these beings had originally evolved from aquatic life, but their current physical appearance was designed and created by the Guoke people.

On their home planet, the males are tiny, living within the bodies of the females. Since their world is mostly covered by water, encounters between males and females are rare. During their evolution, whenever a female encountered a male in the depths of the sea, she would capture him ruthlessly and never allow him to escape. Even after they developed advanced technology and the ability to create their own bodies, many retained the tradition of females capturing males and allowing them to live parasitically inside them.

Norton then announced, "We will soon visit these amphibious parasitic beings and bring them a gift." As he said this, he glanced at me. "And that gift is you, brother."

What?! They planned to offer my body as a gift for these beings to experience, turning me into data for Norton and his team to generate digital wealth?

Norton had a habit of deceiving me or not informing me of his plans in advance, often arranging for me to be unexpectedly subjected to the strange women of the Guoke system. They would use my body for their experiments, often subjecting me to rough treatment. Why was he telling me this so plainly now? Was it because these amphibious beings resembled Earth women, making me less likely to resist? Or maybe these advanced beings were supposed to be civil, gentle, and wouldn't attack or mistreat me.

But I had no right to refuse and feared Norton and his team, so I remained silent.

Soon enough, Norton led us to the place where the amphibious beings resided. From above, we hovered over a ring-shaped island. The scenery was beautiful, with all the necessary facilities, and in the center was a clear body of water.

We descended through the global transportation network and entered an underwater area where, surprisingly, we were surrounded by air rather than water. The place was filled with intricately designed structures and grand buildings. I looked up and saw water, about as high as a ten-story building, seemingly floating without any visible glass or support.

The water floated like clouds in the sky, and fish swam above our heads, casting shadows on the ground below. The sunlight filtered through the shifting water, creating a magical, dreamlike atmosphere.

I could tell that this was a high-end location, fitting for such an advanced species. A virtual digital host greeted us — a beautiful and dignified woman with an alluring face and a voluptuous figure, but she was entirely naked. She floated in the air without touching the ground, about the same height as Weili, and didn't display any signs of being a giant.

I assumed her virtual form could be resized as needed. Her name, translated by the global information network, was "Warmth." Despite her soft and warm appearance, her left hand was replaced by a shiny metal hook, which seemed completely out of place. What did that symbolize?

The virtual host summoned two robots, who spoke with Norton. Norton instructed me to follow them into a room, saying they needed to thoroughly clean my body inside and out.

During my time in the Guoke system, I had encountered many women, all of whom had a penchant for invading my body in various barbaric ways, often with a cruel, sadistic streak. While some of these experiences brought moments of pleasure, most were filled with pain, fear, and nausea, not to mention a sense of being violently mistreated.

Hearing that Norton planned to offer me as a gift to the amphibious beings made me both anxious and curious. The virtual images of the amphibious beings resembled Earth women, and I had long wondered what it would be like to have a real encounter with a gentle, affectionate woman from Earth.

But as soon as Norton mentioned cleaning my body inside and out, my fear returned. Were they preparing me to be eaten?

Previously, I'd had a nightmare where I was captured by primitive savages, who thoroughly cleaned my body inside and out, then seasoned me before roasting me alive. Fortunately, that nightmare had ended quickly.

I entered the room, which seemed virtual at first. As I stepped inside, a large opening appeared, and once I was through, the opening vanished. The room was dimly lit, and I felt a soft, rubbery surface beneath my feet. Sticky liquid droplets fell from the ceiling onto my bare skin, and soon, bright lights illuminated the space.

Several black, flexible tubes shot down from above, spraying soapy water over my body. One of the tubes shaved off my body hair, leaving only a short amount of hair on my head and eyebrows. Another tube sucked on my fingers and toes, quickly grinding away my nails.

The process was quick, and soon my body was thoroughly cleaned on the outside. A tube then extended into my mouth, spraying foamy water inside me. The constant influx of water and pressure made my stomach and intestines feel uncomfortable.

A black ring descended from above, wrapping around my body from head to toe. I felt an intense pressure as yellowish waste was forced out from my bowels and pale urine streamed from my penis. Only when the excretions ran clear, and the black ring reached the floor, did the cleansing finally stop.

Just as I was starting to feel some relief, the rubbery surface beneath me began to melt, and I found myself sinking deeper. Eventually, I fell through a spiral, extremely slippery chute and landed on the ground below.

When I stood up, I found myself surrounded by four massive, naked women. They resembled humans, but their skin was extraordinarily smooth and white, with faint traces of blue, like finely polished porcelain. Their backs were jet black, with a natural transition between the white and black areas.

These women stood about five or six meters tall—true giants. Their bodies were not only tall but also incredibly robust and voluptuous, with two massive breasts the size of large pumpkins, each over half a meter in diameter.

Their nipples were a deep reddish-purple, surrounded by several rings of scales, like those found on fish. Their navels were as large as my head, and their thighs were enormous, each as thick as a tree trunk.

I was stunned by their immense size and found it both awe-inspiring and terrifying. Despite having some idea that they could absorb a male into their bodies, I hadn't expected them to be this overwhelming in real life.

These women were not only massive but also strikingly beautiful. Their long hair resembled seaweed, extending down their spines, and their arms and thighs were adorned with clusters of tentacle-like appendages, resembling catfish whiskers. These women radiated an intense, pungent odor, a combination of raw fish and sour stench that made me want to gag.

One of them picked me up like a mother holding a baby, her skin feeling both smooth and hard. She kissed me, her deep purple lips sparkling with blue highlights, while her sharp, tiny teeth reminded me of a shark's terrifying maw.

Her tongue was made up of many strands, much like the tentacle-like appendages under their arms, resembling hundreds of writhing snakes inside her mouth. She shoved my head into her mouth, and as I opened my eyes, it felt like I was gazing at a night sky dotted with countless blue stars. Her snake-like tongues coiled around my head, covering me with mucus that resembled snot, and the stench was unbearable.

She held me tightly, turning me upside down, pressing me against her body. As I slid downward, rubbing against her slick, smooth skin, the pungent odor, a mix of fishy and sour smells, grew more intense. It was clear that these smells were coming from her lower body.

Her lower body appeared similar to a human woman's, though the color of her skin was uniform throughout. Her lower region was densely covered with long, soft tubes that concealed a narrow slit. The fleshy lips on either side were plump and extended from the front to the back. These tubes grew externally and couldn't retract or extend like Weili's, whose tubes could hide inside her body and retract when not in use.

I later realized that these giants had internal tubes as well. The ones on her body were coiled together like a cluster of strange snakes, writhing continuously. As she moved my body toward her lower region, she completely ignored my instinctive revulsion to the strong, pungent odor.

The other three giant women drew near, completely naked, showing no signs of shame. They spat on me, spreading their legs as long, crimson tubes extended from their lower bodies, shooting sticky, foul-smelling mucus onto me from above. One of them even squeezed the tip of her tube to add more force to the spray.

After covering me from the front, they turned around, bent over, and shook their hips vigorously, swinging their lower tubes in the air, continuing to spray me with thick mucus. My entire body was covered in the viscous liquid, some of it trailing in long, sticky strands as it dripped.

The giant woman then forced my head into her lower body's tube, where the muscles contracted powerfully, creating a strong suction like someone swallowing food. I struggled desperately, afraid that I would suffocate if she fully engulfed me. But it was futile—she easily pulled me inside, where I felt the slimy tubes rub and twist around my head and face.

Fortunately, she soon pulled my head back out. I looked at myself and saw that I was covered in mucus, a thick, white fluid tinged with yellow, clinging to my body. As it dripped down, it stretched into long, unbreakable strands. The sticky nature of the liquid was undeniable.

The intense, strange fishy odor, mixed with the sour smell, reminded me of rotting lobsters, though not entirely. It seemed this foul liquid was the source of the stench. I realized she wasn't done with me yet. Sure enough, she stuffed my feet into her lower body's muscular tube again, and the suction dragged me deeper despite my resistance.

Inside, I encountered an oval-shaped ring of muscle. Its vertical distance was greater than its horizontal, so my arms were trapped outside, and my body couldn't fully enter. The muscles contracted with immense force, pulling me inward, but I remained stuck in an extremely uncomfortable position.

At this moment, the global information network opened, and I heard the familiar voice of the AI assistant, Kewen.

"Poor alien, your body has been imprisoned and is about to endure crushing and grinding pressure. I suggest you try to fall asleep to reduce your pain."

Kewen provided me with visual information, allowing me to see the woman who had absorbed me into her body. She had her eyes closed, mouth wide open, clearly enjoying herself. I understood that she was deliberately using her body to crush and press against mine to heighten her own pleasure.

Many strange women from the Guoke system shared this trait. The pressure was becoming unbearable, so I twisted my body sharply, managing to slip entirely inside, instantly relieving the discomfort.

The inside of her body was the same deep purple-red color as her mouth, with blue specks of light sparkling within. I watched as the opening between two fleshy curtains began to close, causing my heart to race with fear. Fortunately, the gap stopped closing before I was completely trapped.

I could see the thin sliver of light outside through the crack in the flesh, and while my mouth was stuffed with a tube that resembled a pig intestine, the foul odor was overwhelming. However, I could still breathe, and with the suction stopped, I felt somewhat relieved. I reasoned that the terrible stench was preferable to suffocation.

Initially, I thought that this giant woman had only absorbed me into her body for a short time and would eventually let me go. After all, I still needed to relieve myself daily. But I was wrong. She kept me inside for a long time and began to torment me with strange tricks.

Before long, a thick tube forced its way into my rectum, growing inside me. I couldn't see what was happening, but I could feel it moving through my body, pressing and twisting as it traveled.

At first, there was only one tube, but soon I felt several. They invaded my colon, intestines, urethra, and stomach, eventually reaching my throat and mouth. I opened my mouth and spat out a purple-red tube, my heart pounding in fear.

At that moment, I felt her body begin to rhythmically contract around me. The tube in my urethra pulsated, sending waves of intense pleasure through me, unlike anything I had ever experienced. This sensation lasted a long time, far longer than any pleasure I had known before.

I drifted in and out of sleep, but unlike previous experiences, the pleasure didn't fade when I woke. Even in my dreams, I felt that same overwhelming joy, as if it was coming from the tubes filling and pressing against my rectum, urethra, and intestines.

For days — perhaps even longer — I existed in a half-conscious state, consumed by vivid hallucinations and the sensation of pleasure coursing through my body. At that point, I remembered something Norton had once said: when a giant female parasitic species absorbs a male and engages in sexual activity, the pleasure it brings is rated a ten, compared to the mere one of a normal sexual encounter with a human.

But Norton had also warned that the pain inflicted by these giant parasitic species could be the greatest of all, lasting longer and hurting more than anything else. As I reflected on this, a sense of terror crept over me once again.

I suspected that the overwhelming pleasure I was experiencing came from two sources: first, my entire body was encased inside her, allowing her flesh to stimulate me from all angles. Second, the tubes she had inserted into me were likely injecting some kind of toxin that produced the blissful hallucinations.

Her scent, which had repulsed me at first, had now become something I craved. Astonishingly, she had taken full control of my body. Through the tubes, she supplied me with nutrients and oxygen, while simultaneously removing my waste. I had thought I would at least be released for basic bodily functions, but once again, I was wrong.

Instead, I remained in a head-down, feet-up position, only occasionally glimpsing the sliver of light outside as her body tightly encased me. Inside, the invasive tubes left me powerless to resist. My previous feelings of fascination toward these supposedly civilized and intelligent amphibians were completely shattered, replaced by the certainty that they were far more savage and crueler than I had ever imagined.

My fears were confirmed when, after a long time, a powerful force squeezed me out of her body. For a moment, I was hopeful that she might finally release me. But to my horror, she simply pushed my head into the body of another giant woman, subjecting me to the same relentless squeezing and grinding.

They continued to exchange me back and forth like a plaything, showing no intention of stopping. The global information network provided images of them, and I could see they were thoroughly enjoying themselves.

I knew I couldn't fight back — these women were far too powerful. I realized that resistance was futile, so I tried to will myself into unconsciousness. But it was difficult. The rapid, forceful rubbing and crushing of my body left me utterly exhausted. I began to experience hallucinations, feeling as though I was on the verge of death.

Finally, they stopped, and I fell asleep inside her. When I woke, I dreamed that I had been released, resting comfortably in her arms as we basked in the sun. It was a peaceful, joyful, and harmonious feeling. But a sudden jolt woke me from my dream, and I realized I was still trapped inside her body.

She had jumped into the cold ocean, the freezing water splashing against my face. The moment the water hit, the light outside vanished, and I was once again surrounded by darkness. I knew that the narrow sliver of light had been closed off by her body as she swam through the sea.

The global information network kept me informed, showing her and the other three giant women, all naked, swimming gracefully beneath the ocean. Despite their enormous size, they moved through the water with agility and elegance.

I remained inside her, head down and feet up, for so long that blood began to pool in my head, causing dizziness and severe ear ringing. I felt immense discomfort and anxiety, desperately wanting to escape from her body.

Unable to leave on my own, I tried to sleep to cope with the unbearable pressure and anxiety. I drifted in and out of consciousness, filled with strange dreams and buried memories. Time inside her body felt excruciatingly long, as if I had been trapped for years, endlessly wandering the depths of the ocean, witnessing bizarre and dangerous underwater landscapes

Could it be that in a past life I lived like this, deep in the ocean on another planet? And now, I've unlocked the memories of that former existence?

During that time, I had many dreams, the most frequent of which involved me being inside a giant, sticky oil tank. A slippery, fleshy tube would enter my mouth and exit through my rectum, stretching infinitely between the heavens and the earth. My body would slowly glide along this tube, sometimes sliding downward, sometimes rising upward. The thick tube would rub against my throat, intestines, and rectum, producing a strangely pleasant sensation.

In another dream, I was completely naked, sliding down a slick, fleshy tunnel, with that same slippery tube threading through me from mouth to rectum. I found myself sliding between two tubes of varying thickness, moving slowly between them.

Yet another recurring dream involved me swimming in a strange sea, where the water was like thick, transparent oil. No matter how hard I swam upward, I could never reach the surface, so I was forced to swim horizontally. Occasionally, I would encounter a cluster of snake-like beings, a mix of snakes, eels, octopuses, and women. When they touched me, they immediately coiled around me—some wrapped around my legs, some around my neck, and some around my waist. Many of them even slithered into my body through my mouth and rectum, only to slide back out again, over and over, giving me an incredibly smooth, pleasurable sensation with no trace of fear or pain.

When I wasn't dreaming inside her, I fantasized about escaping her body and regaining my freedom, but she never let me out.

I dreamed countless times that I had already escaped, feeling immense relief, only to wake up and find that I was still trapped, staring at the familiar sight of the narrow slit between the fleshy curtains that blocked my exit. My mouth and nose were filled with her tubes, and the hope I had felt quickly turned to despair and hopelessness.

Perhaps the extended time spent upside down, or maybe the way she had replaced my blood or injected some kind of toxin into me, had caused my vision to change. Everything I saw appeared tinted in shades of red and yellow, and everything was blurry, indistinct.

Finally, there was one occasion when she released me. She lay on a virtual couch with her eyes closed, placing me on her lap. The sunlight was warm, and the scenery around me was breathtakingly beautiful, though dazzling to my eyes, likely because I hadn't seen sunlight for so long.

I tried to crawl off her lap, eager to escape. But I couldn't stand. I tried several times, only to fail. My body felt as though it was fractured into pieces that couldn't coordinate with each other. I silently cursed myself, thinking, *how could I fail to escape when I finally have the chance? Why can't I walk now?*

Then I realized that I could still crawl. I began to crawl away, but I hadn't gone far before I felt a sharp pain in my internal organs, as a tube still connected my rectum to her body. With no choice, I returned in defeat.

Since the moment I was captured, I had never truly been free of her body. Even moments like this, basking in the sunlight, were rare.

Norton, Weili, and the others had warned me, and they were right. These amphibious women were insatiably greedy, domineering, and cruel. Once they captured a man and absorbed him into their bodies, they would lock him inside forever, never letting him escape.

At first, I had eagerly hoped she would release me, but over time, I grew terrified of the thought. Each time she squeezed me out partially, revealing my upper body, my heart would be filled with overwhelming dread.

This was because her primary reason for releasing me was to provide entertainment for the other three giant women. She would often press hard, forcing my upper body to emerge from her, and the other women would gather around, spitting on me. They would also spray me with foul, sticky fluids from the long, crimson tubes emerging from their lower bodies.

After covering me in thick mucus, one of them would then pull me into her own lower body, absorbing my upper half. Since I was still connected to the first woman by a tube, they were able to keep me alive, ensuring that I wouldn't suffocate. They likely even used an external system to supply oxygen to my body.

Once my upper half was inside the second woman, they would begin to rub and press against me again. Sometimes, the other two giant women would insert their own tubes, wrapping around my abdomen and squeezing tightly, while another tube would force its way into my rectum, even though I was already connected to the first woman. They didn't care. They would press harder and harder, generating intense pressure inside me.

Sometimes, when they inserted a tube into my urethra, it would swell, while another tube would tightly wrap around my penis, squeezing hard. This inside-out pressure was excruciating.

At times, they would continue torturing me for hours without pulling my upper body out. They enjoyed the pressure and the friction — it must have brought them some kind of twisted pleasure — but I could barely endure it. Every time, I felt as though I was on the verge of death.

I would shout at them, but they never seemed to understand me, nor did they care. I never received a response.

In my mind, I silently begged, *please, I can't take it anymore, just let me go*. I hoped that Kewen from the global information network would somehow transmit my plea to these giants, but nothing happened.

During those moments, I worried that even if I managed to escape, I might not be able to walk. That was a serious concern.

I suspected that the last time I had been freed from her body, my inability to walk was due to the tubes that had been inserted inside me. These tubes were likely preventing me from standing, like a stiff rod placed inside an eel, preventing it from bending.

I didn't just hope to escape from the giant woman's body—I also longed for all her tubes to be fully removed from me, so I could see if I could stand again.

If I couldn't stand, I thought, I'd be as good as useless. Returning home, unable to work, I'd become a burden on my family. Who would care for me? My parents had farm work, and while my grandparents could help, what would happen when they grew too old?

At that point, death would be preferable to such a life. I might as well stay inside her forever.

Then, the opportunity came. She finally released me, pulling out the reddish, mucus-covered tubes from my body. The sticky fluids spilled onto the ground, shining yellowish in the light.

I was shocked to see how thick the tube was that had been pulled from my rectum, while the one from my urethra was much thinner but incredibly long—at least one or two meters in length.

That long? I thought in disbelief, no wonder my bladder and urethra had felt so full.

With the tubes removed, I was left with a strange feeling, as if part of my body had been cut away, leaving me with deep discomfort.

The constant sensation of being filled by the tubes had become so ingrained that when they were gone, my rectum, urethra, and intestines felt empty and uneasy, like my body had grown accustomed to their presence.

Even though I tried my hardest, I still couldn't stand. A wave of despair washed over me.

Just as I was about to collapse, another giant woman, also naked, came over and supported me. As she held me, a tube extended from her lower body, spraying me with more sticky fluids.

I suspected that this giant woman wanted to absorb me into her body as well. They were simply passing me around, with no real intention of letting me go.

I braced myself, knowing that if she absorbed me, I would once again endure the painful friction and pressure inside her body.

Sure enough, she intended to absorb me, though her approach was different. Instead of pulling me in directly, she first inserted a tube into my rectum, then followed it with another one into my mouth.

Several other giant women approached, using their lower-body tubes to bind me in place. One of them even began massaging my penis with her tube.

Gradually, my penis became erect, my arms feeling strong. But why couldn't I stand?

The weakness in my legs felt entirely different from the kind caused by illness. When sick, the whole body weakens, but now it was as if my limbs couldn't coordinate with each other.

I wondered if destroying my penis would cause them to lose interest in me. Perhaps these giant women weren't fixated on human men's genitals, but instead were fascinated by our entire bodies.

The tube from her lower body threaded through my mouth, down into my stomach and intestines, injecting a large quantity of viscous fluid. It then emerged from my rectum, before exploring between my legs and finally wrapping around my penis, squeezing tightly, and then extending into my urethra.

This time, because she had already injected so much fluid into my stomach and intestines, the tube moved easily through my body, threading from my rectum all the way to my mouth, branching off and spreading to other parts of my body.

Then, she began retracting her tube, pulling me toward her. She spread her legs wide and absorbed me into her body, headfirst this time, with my feet the last to disappear. Inside, I could still breathe with no difficulty.

Sometimes, they would release my entire body, and all four of them would extend thick tubes from their lower bodies, attaching them to my limbs and gradually consuming me. They would stop at my armpits and the tops of my thighs, then squeeze me tightly. If my head were absorbed this way, the pressure would be unbearable, and I would scream, but it was always in vain — they never responded.

And so, they continued to exchange me like this, passing me from one to another.

It was only with the help of Norton and the others that I finally managed to escape from the bodies of these giant amphibious women.

When I first emerged, I noticed that the colors of the outside world had returned to normal, though I still couldn't walk. My body felt as though it had been broken into segments that couldn't function together. I was filled with anxiety. I struggled for a while and eventually managed to stand with great effort. Norton reassured me, saying that everything would be fully healed.

At the time, I thought Norton was just trying to comfort me, so I replied, "I'll be satisfied as long as I can walk again."

However, Norton and the others quickly healed me completely, leaving no side effects. I regained my strength, feeling full of energy once more, and my anxiety melted away.

Sometime later, Norton asked if I had noticed any changes in my body. I said no, but then he reminded me about the smell. Only then did I realize that I still carried the strong, fishy odor of the giant amphibious women on my skin and in my mouth.

It felt as if my entire body, inside and out, had been soaked in oil. My skin was now smooth and oily to the touch, and even my internal organs—my intestines, stomach, throat, esophagus, and urethra—felt lubricated. I even noticed that defecating had become much easier.

In the years that followed, I often experienced ringing in my ears. Had it all started back then?

When I mentioned the strange dreams I'd been having, Norton explained that this was a form of "dream control" commonly used by the Guoke people, and that the giant woman had intentionally induced these dreams in me.

Norton went on to explain, "We Guoke people often control others through beauty—attractiveness and an elegant figure. This is like what you experience on Earth. Another method commonly used on your planet is controlling others through wealth, but this doesn't exist on Guoke, because material resources here are free."

He continued, "A more unique method for us is scent control, especially used by females. They can emit powerful, unpleasant odors, but these smells are special. After being exposed to them for a while, the affected person can become addicted to the scent, growing fond of it and even craving it. Everyone's scent is unique.

"There's also toxin control. Many species on Guoke store a wide variety of toxins within their bodies. They can release these toxins suddenly or inject them into someone, causing hallucinations and gaining control over them. This method is brutal and quick, capable of overpowering someone before they can even react.

"Because we have a global movement network, anyone sensing danger can request an instant relocation. But the speed of the toxin injection can often be faster than someone's ability to request a transfer.

"Sometimes, if the toxin levels are low, the global network can remotely replenish them in the body of the attacker.

"Another method involves using tubes from within our bodies to invade another's body, seizing control in a simple and crude manner that often causes pain.

"Certain small parasitic species can enter the body entirely, while larger parasitic species can absorb smaller individuals into themselves. This form of control is violent and direct.

"One of the most common methods on our planet is dream control, which is done through the global information network. A person can imagine various dreamscapes and allow someone else, even at a great distance, to enter these dreams. In this way, they can exert control over the other person."

Norton continued, "This is the most advanced form of control, and it's quite common on Guoke. However, failure is also possible. Sometimes, dream control only lasts for a short while, and other times the person being controlled can even reverse the situation, gaining control of the original dreamer."

He added, "If a giant parasitic species becomes too brutal or keeps someone trapped inside them for too long, causing excessive suffering, the global information network will assess the situation and allow the victim to die. Their consciousness will then be transferred to a new body.

"But if the parasitic species wish to keep their host alive, they must improve their level of dream control. The most skilled at dream control are these giant parasitic species."

Norton also warned me that the giant woman might have left something inside my body. At the time, I didn't pay much attention to his warning.

One night, I had a dream in which I returned to my hometown, resuming my old work of catching eels. I saw a small, finely made tunnel, like a plastic pipe, filled with eels. The tunnel wasn't big, so I crawled inside, catching so many eels that I had to remove my clothes to carry them.

Suddenly, the eels transformed into slender, beautiful women—just like the snake-women I had encountered in the ocean, a hybrid of eels, snakes, and women. They coiled around my body, tightly wrapping my arms, legs, and neck. I panicked and regretted removing my clothes. I yelled, "What do you want?"

I feared they were like the snake-women I had encountered underwater, intending to invade my body. Then, I felt something enter my rectum, and I immediately woke up, finding myself lying on a virtual bed in a well-decorated room, not in the tunnel.

However, I still felt something moving inside my rectum and abdomen. I spread my legs and used my willpower to expel it. Sure enough, a slender snake-like being slowly emerged from my rectum, its body covered in red, green, and black ringed patterns, like those of a venomous snake.

When had this snake-like parasite entered my body? Was it during that dream, or had it happened in this very room while I was asleep?

Over time, I had many encounters with parasitic species. Smaller parasitic women frequently entered my body, while larger ones would absorb me entirely into theirs.

On several occasions, when I emerged from a giant's body, I was shocked to find leech-like creatures in my urethra, alive and wriggling.

Norton later explained that these creatures had been left in my body by the giant woman. Sometimes, I would even see fleshy tubes emerging from my mouth or rectum, resembling chicken intestines, snakes, or octopus tentacles—all of them alive.

Chapter 36: The Purple Mud World

One day, Norton casually mentioned to us that he wanted to take a trip to an underground mud world. He led the way, and soon enough, I found myself with him, Weili, and Sudair, traveling via the Global Transport Network. We arrived at a peculiar spot—no buildings, just a landscape filled with trees, grassy patches, and deep purple swamps. It was likely still on Guoke Planet. If we were headed to another planet, we'd probably have used a UFO.

Instead of landing, we hovered mid-air, cruising while standing, searching for a place to descend. The trees below were all of the same variety, their broad, bright yellow-green leaves showing parallel stripes, and none of them appeared wilted. The vegetation was vibrant, with large, round leaves — no dead ones in sight. Even the grass lacked the fine, pointed blades I was used to.

The ground was divided into segments by what looked like earthen embankments, enclosing purple swamplands. The swamps were pockmarked with countless small holes, each about half a meter wide. Around every hole, a pale purple ring of mud had built up, giving the place an almost surreal appearance.

Suddenly, a digital avatar appeared in front of us — a virtual tour guide in the form of a half-human, half-serpent creature. Her oversized head gave her an almost comical resemblance to a sperm cell or a tadpole. With no legs, her coiled tail acted like a spring, bouncing playfully as she moved. Alongside her floated some Guoke text, which Kewen, our

Global Information Network assistant, translated as *"A Silken Thread."*

Was it supposed to symbolize the slender beauty of women here, their bodies as sinuous as a thread? Perhaps.

Norton and the others, unfazed by the virtual avatar, ignored her and dove straight into one of the mud holes. As they contacted the purple sludge, their virtual clothes vanished, revealing their bare forms for just a moment before they disappeared into the mud below.

I hesitated, fearful of suffocation. Rather than jumping in, I landed cautiously on the embankment, walking around the edges and testing the purple mud with my foot. It felt just like Earth's mud— sticky and soft.

Standing near one of the holes, I debated whether to take the plunge. Just then, Kewen reassured me that I wouldn't suffocate. The Global Transport Network would automatically supply my body with oxygen. With newfound confidence, I dove into the mud. It was surprisingly smooth and silky, not a single grain of sand or stone rubbing against me. The temperature was nearly identical to my body's warmth, and I soon found myself sliding faster and faster through the mud.

The tunnel sloped downward, and after what felt like an eternity, I arrived in a massive underground chamber bathed in soft, purple light. Looking up, I saw the tiny tunnel I had just slid through, its entrance dripping with mud. Oddly enough, the mud didn't fall as gravity would dictate. Perhaps Guoke's technology, or the Global Network itself, held it in place.

The chamber I had entered stretched horizontally, about three to four meters high and five to six meters wide, with no visible end in sight. I tried walking, but the ground was uneven, like a bowl, and covered with thick, slippery mud, making movement nearly impossible. Kewen suggested I slide instead, which worked effortlessly.

It felt as though I was gliding on thought alone—wherever I wanted to go, my body simply followed. Even uphill, the sliding felt natural, as if an unseen force was helping me along. As I slid, I noticed several side tunnels branching off from the main chamber, some above, some below, and some along the sides.

At Kewen's direction, I ventured into one of the lower tunnels, which led to yet another large horizontal chamber. There were dozens of layers, she told me. After some exploration, I returned to the first level, continuing to slide until I entered a vast space, dimly lit by the same purple glow.

This world was filled with bizarre lifeforms. Strange plants, a pale green yellow in color, contrasted against the purple background, while snake-like creatures and humanoids slithered and swam through the mud. It felt as though I had entered a surreal dreamscape.

Kewen explained that Guoke people would come here to live for extended periods. They preserved their original bodies in a kind of time-stasis and switched into snake-like forms better suited for navigating this muddy underworld. Those who came for shorter visits, like us, didn't bother with body swaps.

Indeed, many of the beings I saw were in their original Guoke forms, although others had fully adopted their snake-like bodies. They were all naked, yet their mud-covered forms made their nudity less noticeable. I looked down and realized my virtual clothes had disappeared too.

These serpent people, much like the ones I had seen in the ocean, were long and slender, with sleek, shiny bodies. Their waists were impossibly thin, and they possessed arms but no legs — their lower halves extended into snake-like tails. Some of the females had long, pointed breasts and genitalia, and their hands were more like fish fins than human appendages.

They had human faces, but their eyes were elongated, slanting upward at a sharp 45-degree angle, with small, gleaming pupils. Their mouths and noses were tiny, giving them an eerie, almost mischievous appearance. Their bodies came in vibrant shades — crimson, emerald, jet black — and some were covered in intricate patterns, resembling living works of art.

I stayed away from them. Although their slick, shining bodies were alluring, I had learned enough from past encounters to know better than to get too close.

Closing my eyes, I imagined what would happen if I caught their attention. I could already picture them swarming me, coiling around me with their snake-like bodies, their appendages eagerly probing every inch of my body for an entry point. In no time, my nose, mouth, and even my backside would be invaded by those probing tentacles. At first, it would feel exhilarating, but soon their rapid, relentless pace would wear me down, leaving me utterly drained.

No, I wouldn't survive that.

Still, my curiosity got better of me. I ventured further, sliding through tunnels, until suddenly, I bumped into someone in the darkness. Immediately, they wrapped themselves around me — a slender figure with a cold, smooth body. Judging by her slim waist and delicate features, I could tell it was a woman. Her skin was hard but sensuously smooth, and the sensation was both exhilarating and terrifying.

Her waist felt as thin as my arm, and although her limbs were slender, they held surprising strength as she wrapped herself tightly around me. My hands roamed her body, feeling her long, firm breasts and narrow hips. Her lower half was a single, continuous tail, much like a snake's.

I was tempted to engage with her, thinking she was alone and not a threat, but every time I tried to initiate something, her body twisted and coiled, preventing me from getting any closer. It was as if she was teasing me, and yet, I couldn't figure out her true intentions.

Eventually, she led me to a larger underground chamber. Here, the space opened into a conical room, faintly lit by purple light. In the center, a ring of earth formed a seat, and we sat down together. As I examined her more closely, I realized she had scarlet skin with lighter red across her abdomen. Dozens of thin, violet-red tentacles sprouted from her lower body, wriggling in anticipation.

Suddenly, she climbed onto me, her tentacles wrapping around my neck and inserting themselves into my mouth. Despite the strangeness of the sensation, there was something undeniably pleasurable about the way they moved inside me. My stomach churned with excitement and fear as I wondered if her tentacles would pierce through me, but when I felt the liquid ooze out of my backside, I realized she had released me.

For a while, she continued to coil around me, her body tightening in waves, her tentacles squeezing, but the experience left me feeling only pleasure and no pain. Eventually, I drifted off to sleep. When I awoke, she was gone.

Fearing that she might return with others, I quickly slid away, grateful for the blissful encounter but not eager for a repeat with her kind.

Though the experience had left me physically exhausted, it had also filled me with an overwhelming sense of satisfaction — a rare instance of intimacy in this strange world that didn't end in torment.

As I continued sliding through the tunnels, I remained cautious, avoiding the serpent women wherever possible. I'd learned my lesson before and wasn't keen on testing their boundaries again.

Later, I stumbled upon an enormous conical chamber, far larger than any I had seen before. At the center was a giant lotus-like plant, its glowing petals radiating a soft blue hue. The lotus's center resembled a seed pod, surrounded by dozens of sleek, glowing tendrils that waved in the air like the heads of tiny tadpoles.

Drawn in by curiosity and the strange fragrance that filled the room, I decided to sit on the lotus pod, imagining myself like a Buddha seated in meditation. But the moment I sat down, the tendrils began to move. I realized too late that the plant was alive, and I was caught in its trap. A strong, intoxicating scent filled the air, making my head spin, and before I knew it, my body felt weak and my mind clouded. The tendrils started to wrap around me, and soon I felt a sharp pressure against my skin.

Then, I felt something strange — an intrusion. The tendrils were not just wrapping around me; they were penetrating me. One of the thicker tendrils had found its way into my body through my mouth, filling my stomach with a strange warmth. More tendrils followed, sliding under my skin, exploring my insides as they expanded and pulsed with an eerie rhythm.

Panic set in, but I couldn't move. My body was paralyzed, and I could only watch as the lotus plant slowly began to encase me in its fleshy petals. I tried to fight the sensation, but the warm, liquid-like substance filling my body from the tendrils brought an unexpected euphoria that dulled my fear.

Just as I thought I would lose myself entirely, a sudden burst of energy jolted through me. The tendrils retracted, and the plant's grip loosened. I collapsed onto the ground, gasping for air. As I looked around, I saw that the serpent figures from earlier were watching from the shadows, their eyes glowing eerily in the purple light.

Somehow, I had managed to escape the full grasp of the lotus, but the feeling of its invasive touch lingered. It was both terrifying and strangely pleasurable—a dangerous blend that made me question my sanity.

Gathering my strength, I knew I couldn't stay here any longer. I slid away as fast as I could, avoiding any further encounters with the strange creatures of this underground world. Eventually, I found my way back to the others.

Norton, Weili, and Sudair were waiting for me, seemingly unfazed by their own experiences in the mud world. They exchanged knowing looks as I joined them, covered in the remnants of the strange encounter I had just endured.

"You'll get used to it," Norton said with a grin, as if he already knew exactly what had happened. "The mud world has a way of getting under your skin."

I nodded, too exhausted to argue, but the experience had left its mark on me. The purple mud world was not just a place of adventure — it was a place where the boundaries of pleasure and fear were dangerously blurred. And as we left, I couldn't help but wonder when — or if — I would return to face it again.

Chapter 37: Meeting the Scientific Titan of Guoke Planet

One day, Norton suggested we visit a renowned scientist on Guoke Planet named Levin. He was as famous here as Einstein is on Earth, having played a pivotal role in the scientific development of Guoke Planet. Levin's contributions spanned physics, mathematics, and philosophy, and his influence stretched across the entire Guoke star system.

Norton had scheduled a meeting with Levin, so we—Norton, Sudair, Weili, and I—used the Global Movement Network to visit a science exchange center on Guoke Planet. We waited in a room for Levin's arrival. While we waited, Norton, Sudair, and Weili began talking about Levin, and I could tell they deeply admired him.

"In Guoke Planet, or really the whole Guoke star system, those who control the fate of our people are scientists like Levin," Norton explained. "Though the Global Movement Network and the Global Information Network have made life easier for everyone, they've also created a heavy dependency on them. Without these two networks, Guoke people wouldn't be able to survive. In essence, we're ruled by science, and our destiny is shaped by scientists like Levin. Through him, we gain access to more resources from Guoke Planet."

Norton continued, "I've spoken with Levin over the Global Information Network before, but I've never met him in person. The last time I sent him information about you, he agreed to this meeting. So, thanks to you, we're finally getting this chance!"

It was clear that Norton held Levin in high regard, as did Weili and Sudair. I, on the other hand, was indifferent, picturing Levin as a typical Einstein-like figure in my mind.

Not long after, Levin suddenly appeared before us. To my surprise, he looked quite ordinary. He was about the same height as Norton and the others, resembling a young boy with a kind face. The only unusual feature was his eyebrows — they were dark and looked drawn on, tightly sticking to his face, unlike most Guoke people who had short, faint, or even invisible eyebrows.

Norton and the others stood up to greet Levin, using a gesture like what we do on Earth. They placed their right hand on their chest and lightly patted each other's shoulders with their left hand — a form of greeting I hadn't seen before.

Despite Levin's status, he didn't carry himself with the arrogance of a great scientist. He quickly engaged Norton and Sudair in an animated conversation. Although they had many topics to discuss, Levin seemed most interested in me. He turned to Norton and asked, "Why did you bring this Earthling, called Qian, to Guoke Planet?"

When Qian was a child, he encountered a highly advanced alien civilization in an open field. Their technology is likely millions, if not billions, of years ahead of ours," Norton replied. "During this encounter, the aliens somehow infiltrated Qian's consciousness, leaving behind fragments of their knowledge in his brain. We've already conducted experiments and recorded these memories. We plan to analyze them further."

"How did you know these advanced aliens had encountered Qian?" Levin asked.

"We're members of the 'Study of Earthlings' forum on the Global Information Network. Years ago, we set up a system to monitor Earth. Anytime extraterrestrial contact occurs there, our equipment picks it up and automatically tracks the event," Norton explained.

Levin nodded. "That's impressive. Have you found any insights left behind by these advanced aliens that might deepen our understanding of the universe?"

"So far, we've only recorded Qian's memories. We haven't fully analyzed the data yet, but we're hopeful that it contains valuable information," Norton responded.

"You have a rare opportunity now," Sudair said to me. "Why don't you ask him any questions you have about the mysteries of the universe?"

I thought for a moment and then asked, "How did the universe come into being?"

Levin smiled. "That question is flawed. The universe has always existed and will always continue to exist. It has no beginning and no end. Time, as we perceive it, is merely an illusion created by the movement of space at the speed of light. Without an observer, time doesn't exist — there is no before or after."

Sudair added, "On Earth, your scientists believe the universe began with a big bang about 15 billion years ago. But that's incorrect. What happens in certain regions of the universe is that celestial bodies are drawn together by gravity, compressing until they collide with other stars and explode, forming nebulas. These nebulas then evolve into galaxies. It's a continuous cycle, but this process only occurs in localized parts of the universe. The idea that the entire universe began with one big bang is completely wrong."

I followed up with another question. "What is the most profound mystery of the universe? Can it be summed up in one sentence?"

Sudair smiled. "You've just asked about the ultimate theorem of the universe—the highest law."

Levin answered, "In my view, the universe is composed of objects and the space around them. Nothing else exists. Anything beyond that is merely a description we've made of the movement of these objects and the space around them."

He continued, "This is the most fundamental law of the universe, the deepest and highest understanding. All intelligent civilizations, no matter how advanced, eventually arrive at this realization. On any planet with intelligent life, the first person to grasp this truth is often considered a god."

"On Earth, our most famous scientist might have reached this understanding," I said. "Was it Einstein?"

Levin shook his head. "No, it was Galileo. He once said, 'The physical world we perceive through our senses is false; the true reality lies in the geometric world behind it.' This geometric world consists of objects and space. By making such a statement, Galileo showed that he understood that only objects and space truly exist, and everything else — what we call physics — is merely a description of their motion. Without an observer, the physical world doesn't exist, but the geometric world remains."

He added, "Earth's physics was born with Galileo, and perhaps it will end with him when people fully understand his statement that 'the physical world is false.' Once you understand the highest law of the universe, the depth of physics reaches its limit. But mathematics is different — there is no highest law in mathematics. It's infinite, and physics is just a part of it."

"If Galileo understood this, he may have been touched by an advanced alien civilization. Otherwise, I can only assume he was a god in the universe," Levin said.

Sudair chimed in, "We plan to turn Qian into such a god on Earth. We'll use field-scanning technology to implant advanced scientific theories into his mind — especially those related to time, space, and fields. He'll become the god of Earth, and we'll be the creators behind him!" Sudair laughed triumphantly.

"But how will you bypass the 'Interstellar Treaty Alliance'?" Levin asked. "That treaty requires the deletion of any advanced technological knowledge from low-level civilizations when they return to their home planets — especially anything related to time, space, or fields."

Levin explained further, "In every intelligent civilization across the universe, the discovery of the nature of fields marks a turning point. Understanding fields means understanding space, time, and forces. This knowledge leads to technologies like instant teleportation, light-speed travel, free energy, and even the artificial field-based immortality you see here on Guoke. These advancements can improve life dramatically but can also cause catastrophic harm."

Norton confidently replied, "We've studied this for a long time. We have ways to bypass the alliance's checks. Our goal is to help Qian bring advanced field-related technology to Earth, making him the 'Levin' of his world."

Levin chuckled. "Earth will enter a new era, driven by forces invisible to the naked eye. Welcome to the age of light-speed travel and interstellar civilization! And behind it all, we'll know it was your work, Norton, Sudair, and Weili!"

Weili teased, "When Qian becomes famous, I'll visit Earth in a flying saucer to see him again."

I couldn't resist joking, "And if I remain obscure, you won't visit?"

Weili laughed. "Who knows? Maybe I'll still come see you."

Levin turned to me. "Even if they implant all this advanced knowledge into your brain, do you think you'll be able to comprehend it and spread it on Earth?"

Norton interjected confidently, "We've been monitoring Qian for a long time. He has the necessary qualities: intelligence, wisdom, and integrity."

Levin nodded. "On Earth, to become a great scientist, one needs three qualities: intelligence, wisdom, and integrity. Intelligence is the ability to quickly absorb, understand, and express knowledge. Wisdom goes beyond that — it's the capacity to deeply process, apply, and innovate upon that knowledge. Integrity allows one to persist in the pursuit of truth."

We discussed many profound topics, ranging from the secrets of space to the nature of light and time. Levin revealed the mysteries of the universe and how it was ultimately tied to the movement of space itself, not time, as I had once thought.

As the conversation ended, Norton assured me, "We'll use artificial field-scanning technology to implant these concepts into your brain. When you need them, they'll emerge naturally. You won't be overwhelmed, but you'll gradually master this knowledge. It's going to be crucial for Earth."

Before we left, we even met a few long-deceased, legendary Guoke scientists, who appeared before us as virtual avatars. Norton mentioned that someday, Earth would also create digital versions of Newton, Galileo, and Einstein to interact with the public.

As we bid farewell to Levin, I felt as if I had touched the core of the universe. And with the knowledge they were planning to implant in my mind, I would soon have the power to reshape my world.

Chapter 38: Guoke Scientists on Consciousness, the Soul, and Reincarnation

A question that had been nagging at me suddenly surfaced: "When we die on Earth, is that really the end? Is reincarnation real? Do we truly have an endless cycle of life?"

Norton responded, "Death is not the end for any human being, whether on Earth or elsewhere in the universe. Yes, reincarnation is real, and the cycle of life is a universal truth. On many planets, people experience life in cycles, just as Earthlings do."

He explained further, "Humans can be divided into two parts: the body and the mind. Your thoughts, consciousness, and awareness are forms of electrical activity in the brain. This activity is essentially information, and information doesn't die — it's not something that can rot away like a body. The body perishes, but the essence, the mind, is a form of movement, an expression of information that can reappear repeatedly throughout the universe.

"The core law of the universe is simple: it must express every form of movement, every possibility, and all information endlessly. That's why reincarnation is real. What you experience on Earth, from birth to death, is just one small part of an infinite cycle of existence. You had past lives, and you will have future lives. This reincarnation isn't a rare phenomenon; it applies to every person and every animal on Earth. In fact, it applies to all beings across the universe who have yet to master the technology of immortality. They all experience this infinite cycle of reincarnation."

Weili chimed in, "Qian, do you know what your past or future lives are?"

I shook my head. "I have no idea."

"Then what exactly is the soul?" I asked.

Norton answered, "The soul is the unique part of your consciousness. While most of a person's thoughts and awareness are like others, around one-fifth is different. That different portion is what makes up your soul. It's the core of your consciousness and distinguishes you from everyone else. Your body is just a vessel for the soul."

Levin added, "Your brain generates electromagnetic waves that can disturb the surrounding space, causing it to ripple. These ripples carry your consciousness and information at the speed of light, spreading them in all directions."

As he spoke, Levin waved his hand, and a three-dimensional hologram appeared, showing a head surrounded by light-like waves radiating outward. He continued, "So, your thoughts and consciousness can be carried by space itself and preserved forever. They won't disappear. The soul is a part of that consciousness and can also be expressed through these waves. The soul is real, and its wave-like nature is one of its key characteristics.

"Because the three-dimensional space we live in compresses into two dimensions at light speed, your soul can instantaneously reach any point in the universe. Information traveling at the speed of light exists in a two-dimensional space. This means that the information from any point in space can be preserved and accessed, holding the past, present, and future all at once."

Levin then delved deeper into his explanation, "In the universe, any given point in space contains all the information about everything that has ever happened and will ever happen. This is the basis of our theory of the universal information field. On Earth, prophets can sometimes predict the future because they have the ability to tap into this hidden information within space."

He explained further, "Time is merely the way we perceive the outward expansion of space at light speed. Without an observer, time doesn't exist. In the absence of humans, all the events of the past and future could theoretically overlap at a single point in space. Space not only stores information but also transmits it. The information carried by space can be accessed from any point—no matter where you are, the information will be the same."

He concluded, "Unlike physical objects, information can overlap within space, meaning that infinite possibilities can coexist. And because the universe follows the core law of expressing all possibilities endlessly, anything—no matter how strange or unusual—will happen at some point, again and again."

I tried to wrap my head around his words. "So, when we reincarnate, where do we go? Could I end up on Guoke Planet?" I asked.

Sudair smiled and shook his head. "No, that's not possible. Guoke people have achieved immortality. You might reincarnate on another less advanced planet, but never here."

"Could we reincarnate as animals, like pigs or cows?" I asked.

Norton replied, "No, that wouldn't happen. The difference in the form of souls between humans and animals is too great."

"Could I reincarnate as a woman?" I asked, genuinely curious.

Norton again shook his head. "No, the form of the soul would be too different. That person wouldn't be you anymore."

I asked another burning question, "If reincarnation is real, does that mean we don't need to fear death?"

Norton answered, "Death causes the complete loss of memory, which is the greatest harm to humans — it's far more significant than the loss of the body. Your innate consciousness is like a warehouse, and your memories are stored goods. The soul is like the worker in the warehouse, managing it all. When you die, your brain decays, and along with it, your memory and soul information. However, this information is stored in space and doesn't completely disappear. The soul remains intact, but it gets separated from your memories."

He continued, "Your consciousness and soul will be stored in space, and when a new life begins, these elements are downloaded back into the body, but without the previous memories."

Curious about my past lives, I asked, "Can you find out who I was in a past life?"

Norton nodded, "Yes, we can access both your past and future lives. Since the universe contains all information, including your past and future, we can use our field-scanning technology to decrypt these hidden details from space. We can even predict your future experiences back on Earth."

He added, "You may wonder how we can access future information when it hasn't happened yet. The answer lies in the nature of time. Time is merely our perception of the outward expansion of space at light speed. Without an observer, all events — past and future — are effectively overlapped in space. In theory, from any single point, you could decipher everything."

Levin jumped in, "Although we can theoretically access this information, it's incredibly challenging to implement. Our research into decoding the future is at the cutting edge of science, requiring the collaboration of our best mathematicians and physicists. It involves complex theories of space, time, and trends — what you might link to calculus on Earth but far more advanced."

Sudair added, "We've also used this research to recover historical images. If Guoke officially contacts Earth, we could show you true images of your past dynasties — the Tang, the Song, and so on. Your history will come to life in ways you never imagined."

"When will you officially contact Earth?" I asked.

"Once you've developed light-speed spacecraft, we'll likely initiate contact," Sudair answered. "At that point, other advanced civilizations will also consider Earth worthy of dialogue. And with your spacecraft zipping around the universe, we'll all run into each other eventually. Better to start the conversation sooner than later."

Chapter 39: Going Home

Finally, Norton brought up the topic of sending me back home. My time on Guoke Planet had been exhilarating and full of unforgettable experiences, but now that it was time to leave, I couldn't help but feel a wave of sadness.

What made me even more melancholic was that only Sudair and Norton would be piloting the spaceship to return me to Earth. Why wasn't Weili coming with me? Norton explained that it was her own decision not to come. Why, though? Was she afraid that saying goodbye would be too painful for her? Had I overestimated my importance in her life? Maybe she'd had many lovers, and I was just another passing fling—a human boyfriend from Earth who didn't mean much. Or perhaps Norton and the others had made the decision for her, offering this as an excuse.

As they prepared for my return, I noticed Norton was particularly meticulous. He seemed deeply concerned about the *Interstellar Alliance Agreement*. He was going over all the details, instructing me on how to evade the Alliance's checks so I could sneak advanced technology related to the field back to Earth. But I couldn't muster the same enthusiasm. My mind was preoccupied with thoughts of Weili. I resented their plan but knew there was no alternative.

In the air, Norton made a quick gesture with his hand, and a virtual image appeared. It was a projection of me, naked, lying on a bed in a room. A figure entered the room, dressed in a full-body suit with a large black tube attached to the back of their head, leading down to their rear. They held something resembling a microphone, pointing it at my head while watching a small virtual screen intently.

Norton explained, "That's their scanner. The *Interstellar Alliance* doesn't use our equipment, so they'll be scanning your brain for residual memories of Guoke Planet. If they detect anything, they'll delete it themselves or ask us to remove it again. When they shine that device on your head, they're looking for traces of your experiences here."

He added, "During their deep scan, you might see flashes of a black box with a sudden bright light in the center—that's their deep detection. But don't worry, we have a way to counter this. I'll insert a continuous stream of alternate consciousness images into your brain right now."

Norton called over two women. Though only about a meter tall, they were incredibly beautiful—more stunning than Weili, with soft, delicate features that resembled human women much more closely. Their skin was a shade close to Earthly human tones, unlike the typical pale pinkish-white and green hues of Guoke people. They didn't have the usual protrusions between their legs that were common on Guoke women, which made them seem even more human-like.

They sat next to me, gently caressing my bare skin. I felt embarrassed, especially with Norton standing there watching, but he didn't seem to mind. "These two have special abilities," Norton explained, "They can hypnotize you and influence your consciousness through space manipulation."

Sure enough, sleep soon overtook me. In my dream, I was back on Earth in my hometown, and the two women had somehow transformed. One had become my mother, and the other was now my wife. They lived harmoniously together, cooking, cleaning, farming, and raising chickens. I was chopping firewood, catching fish, and tending to the crops. Occasionally, the images in my dream would cut out, but then they'd reconnect, continuing the peaceful rural life.

When I woke up, the two women were still beside me. Norton pointed to a three-dimensional screen, showing a scene identical to the dream I had just experienced. "Is this the dream you had?" he asked.

I was astonished. "Yes, it's exactly the same! This is incredible!"

"Perfect!" Norton exclaimed, raising his fists in triumph. "This is exactly the result we needed."

Soon after, Norton and the two women left the room. The officials from the *Interstellar Alliance* arrived, equipped with their scanner, the same microphone-like device from before. As they scanned my head, I saw the black box with a flash of light, just as Norton had described. And once again, the image of the two women, now as my wife and mother, filled my mind.

Everything went smoothly. The *Interstellar Alliance* officials finished their scan and left, and I remained in a semi-conscious state.

I heard the ship's automated voice announce, "Zone 300 spacecraft has initiated autopilot mode." I realized I was on my way back to Earth. But instead of feeling excited, I felt empty. The thrill of exploring Guoke Planet was behind me, and now I was heading back to the mundane life I had left behind. I didn't want to open my eyes—I just lay there, lost in thought.

Suddenly, I heard the sound of women's laughter, a silvery chime that made me open my eyes. I saw Sudair and Norton intently focused on the virtual screen. The laughter came from the two women who had been with me earlier. They were kneeling near my head, still giggling and speaking in a language I couldn't understand. My translator wasn't picking up their words, so I simply watched them curiously.

One of them made a gesture, creating a virtual barrier that separated us from Norton and Sudair. My translator kicked in again, and I could hear their voices. They were talking about how they had helped Norton in exchange for a reward—to experience the body of a human man.

Their faces were filled with a clear desire, unmistakably the kind that any woman—whether on Earth, on Guoke, or even in the depths of the oceans of Mercury—shows when she craves intimacy with a man. They began kissing me, and my virtual clothes quickly disappeared. To my surprise, their bodies lacked the usual bulges between the legs that were common in Guoke women. Instead, they had small red dots, the size of fingertips. I felt a wave of disappointment — how could anything intimate happen with that?

Just as I was about to resign myself to a simple massage, I felt something snake-like moving between my legs. I opened my eyes to find pink, slender tubes, about the thickness of chopsticks, slithering out from the two women's bodies. They wove their way across my skin before slipping into my body, filling me with waves of pleasure. I felt as if I was being entwined by serpents, drifting between dreamlike ecstasy and moments of clarity.

The two women were relentless, draining my energy while they laughed and teased, seemingly unconcerned. They took turns caressing me and each other, their giggles never stopping.

I don't know how long I stayed like that or how I eventually made it home. When I woke up, I was lying naked in my own bed. The sunlight was streaming through the window, and it was morning. I tried to get dressed but couldn't find my shirt or underwear, so I had to grab fresh clothes from the wardrobe.

As I stepped into the main room, the familiar smell of duck droppings filled the air—my mother hadn't let the ducks out yet. She was busy making breakfast. Everything seemed so ordinary, yet strangely different, as though I had been away for years and was now returning to a place that had become unfamiliar.

I stepped outside and saw a neighbor's daughter working nearby. I asked her what day it was. She paused, turned around with a serious expression, and answered simply, "I don't know."